THE ASYLUM - BOOK SEVEN OF BEYOND THESE WALLS

A POST-APOCALYPTIC SURVIVAL THRILLER

MICHAEL ROBERTSON

EDITED AND COVER BY ...

To contact Michael, please email:
subscribers@michaelrobertson.co.uk

Edited by:

Pauline Nolet - http://www.paulinenolet.com

Cover design by The Cover Collection

COPYRIGHT

The Asylum - Book seven of Beyond These Walls

Michael Robertson
© Michael Robertson 2020

The Asylum - Book seven of Beyond These Walls is a work of fiction. The characters, incidents, situations, and all dialogue are entirely a product of the author's imagination, or are used fictitiously and are not in any way representative of real people, places, or things.

Any resemblance to persons living or dead is entirely coincidental.

All rights reserved.

No part of this publication may be reproduced, stored in a retrieval system, or transmitted in any form or by any means electronic, mechanical, photocopying, recording, or otherwise, without the prior written permission of the author except in the case of brief quotations embodied in critical articles and reviews.

READER GROUP

Join my reader group for all my latest releases and special offers. You'll also receive these four FREE books. You can unsubscribe at any time.

Go to www.michaelrobertson.co.uk

CHAPTER 1

William woke up shivering. That had happened a lot lately. The familiar damp press of dew-soaked clothes lay against his skin, his chest frigid, the cool moist night boring into his lungs. He drew a deep breath and coughed with a phlegmy rattle. But at least they'd woken to a new day. At least they were moving into spring, and at least he had Matilda by his side. They'd fallen asleep in each other's arms, but she now sat up, her knees pulled into her chest as she stared out across the wastelands.

Maybe he should have lain there for longer. His body ached from head to toe, and he groaned as he sat up beside her. Her face pale, her brow beaded with what appeared to be dew, he reached across and wiped the moisture away, pausing on her hot forehead. "You're sweating, Tilly."

Matilda pulled her bandage away to show him.

A slow writhe turned through William. The wound, at least an inch deep and eight inches long, now glistened with a milky white pus. "How's it gotten so infected so quickly?"

Matilda shrugged. "Maybe they'd coated the blade with something. Maybe it was just dirty." Bags bulged beneath her glazed brown eyes. She continued to stare out across the grassy meadow, thousands of diseased below them. "And it's not like we can go on a hunt for ointment."

"How fast can you run right now?"

"I'm not sure. But I can feel myself getting slower by the minute."

"Shit!"

"And if I get any diseased blood in it ..."

"We're screwed," William said.

"*I'm* screwed."

"There has to be a way to fix it. There's always a way."

Matilda's full lips thinned from where she pressed them tight. Her brow wrinkled. Positive affirmations were awful painkillers.

Olga and Max were stirring. They'd spent the night close, albeit with their backs to one another. They'd work it out with time.

Hawk had remained on guard on one side of their camp, Cyrus and Artan on the other. They were still staring out across the roof. Had any of them slept?

Hawk approached them. He remained naked from the waist up, his body tight with his bulging muscles. Deep scars slashed across his torso. He wore his wounds like a badge of honour. Just look at how damn tough he was. Although he put William to shame, who continued to shiver while the hunter stood impervious to the cold. As he drew closer, Hawk fixed on the wound on Matilda's thigh. A slight wince narrowed his eyes. The jangle of keys, he reached into his pocket and held up a thick ring on the end of his right index finger. "I need to find a way to get Dianna out of the asylum."

"You have just looked at the cut on Matilda's leg, right?" William said.

Another slight wince, Hawk then pointed at the large

industrial building on the other side of the sea of diseased. "Dianna's in that place. I need to get her out."

After working his jaw, chewing the air in front of him, William said, "Allow me to explain myself more clearly. Screw Dianna."

Hawk's muscles tensed.

"We wouldn't be in this mess if it wasn't for you and your fucked-up community of sycophants and alpha males. You'll forgive us for not prioritising your needs and the needs of those affiliated with Grandfather Jacks."

"Dianna's done nothing wrong."

"Neither's Matilda."

"I can speak for myself, William," Matilda said.

"Then why don't you?"

"I have nothing to say."

"Also"—William leaned to the left to look past Hawk at the asylum—"have you seen the state of that place?"

"It was bad enough with the lights on in there," Matilda said. "It must be hell on earth in the darkness."

"We need to make the best choices for us right now," William said.

"And what about Dianna?" Hawk's pecs twitched and his biceps bulged. Although he spoke with a quiet tone, a low thunder rumbled beneath his words. "She's a victim in all this too. As are the other women in there. You've been inside the place, Matilda."

As pale as ever, still drenched in sweat, Matilda dropped her focus to her lap.

"And what about all the children?"

"Children?" William said.

"The little boys." Hawk's voice wavered while he ran his fingers along the rope burns on his neck. He then traced some of the deeper slashes on his chest and shoulders. An involuntary reaction, his fingers relived the memories of his own suffering like a blind person reading Braille. "His *angels*. How will they fare with the dark insanity inside that place? The screaming, the cold, the damp, that damn noise calling the diseased to the front of the place."

"At least that's stopped," William said.

Hawk shrugged. "Don't you care?"

"I care very much. I care about what's going to happen to Matilda because of what she's been through. I empathise with Dianna and the others, but I'm sorry, they're not my priority."

"William's right." Max had moved closer to the boys. He stood with his feet planted, his legs wide to give him a strong base. He held his war hammer across his front with both hands and glared at the scarred hunter. "Hawk, you've caused this group nothing but trouble since we met you."

"*I* kissed him, Max," Olga said, "not the other way around."

The twist of Max's features ran counter to his words. "You think I give a shit about a pathetic kiss between you two?"

Olga's face reddened. Where she usually fought everything, she stepped back as if shoved by his words.

"You weren't there when we were out hunting," Max said. "When he handed us over to Magma."

Artan and Cyrus joined the group.

Max continued. "It might have done us a favour if you were. You might have been able to keep him distracted so he didn't send us to our death."

"I'm sorry about that," Hawk said. "I wasn't thinking straight." Again he rubbed his neck and chest. "Sometimes I don't think straight."

"Forgive me, Hawk," William said, "but if you can't take responsibility for your own thoughts, how do you expect us to risk our lives helping you?"

"Helping *Dianna*!"

Max clenched his fists at his sides and stepped closer. He bared his teeth when he spoke, his face red. "You're lucky I don't throw you from this roof right now."

"Why don't you?" Another ripple of tensing muscles ran across Hawk's torso. "You'd be doing me a favour. I'm better turned into one of them than standing up here knowing Dianna's suffering and there's nothing I can do to help her."

"If you're so worried about Dianna," Max said, "why did you leave her in there?"

"It's dark enough in that place with the lights on." Hawk's eyes lost focus. "When the power went, the place turned pitch black. I couldn't see a thing. Also, when that damn sound stopped, what was keeping the diseased around the front of the asylum? At some point they were bound to get bored, and … well …" He swept his hand out over the wastelands.

"So you were scared?"

"Worse than scared," Hawk said. "The lack of electricity rendered me utterly impotent. If I waited too long, I would have also been trapped."

"It's bad in there, Max." Olga touched his shoulder, but he pulled away from her. "It was hell with the lights on. I can't even imagine what Dianna's having to go through now. She could be tied up. She might be submerged in water. She has no one to let her out. No one to feed her."

"Why do you care so much?" Max said.

"Dianna was kind to us."

William's stomach sank when Matilda nodded along with Olga. "She untied us when we were bound and helped us understand what we were facing. Without her warnings, I'm not sure we would have gotten out of there."

Max stepped away from Olga's touch, her hand falling limp at her side with a gentle slap. He moved a step closer to

Hawk. No more than two feet separated the boys. Max stood as the taller of the two, although Hawk had pecs like rocks and biceps like baseballs.

The size of the boy didn't deter Max. He put his war hammer down so the head of it rested on the tiles. He removed his top. "Max," William said, "what are you doing? Put your clothes back on, man."

Max scrunched his top into a ball and threw it at Hawk. It hit the boy's wide, scarred chest and fell to the tiles. Instead of watching it, Hawk remained fixed on Max, the sides of his face widening from the tight clench of his jaw.

"You're not a hunter anymore," Max sneered. "You look ridiculous."

Another shimmering wave of tension rippled through Hawk's upper body at Max moving closer. He remained statue still, his glare unwavering when Max pulled the keys from his hand. He turned his back on the boy and stormed off.

"What are you doing?" Olga said.

"Going to the asylum."

Although Olga opened her mouth, she said nothing.

Without looking back, Max jumped down to a lower part of the roof. William stood up and followed the boy, watching his back as he climbed from the roof into the meadow filled with diseased.

Twenty to thirty feet away from the palace, Max spun around at the scream bursting from the building.

Four people emerged: one woman and three men. Hunters by the look of it, the men naked from the waist up. They charged Max, their weapons raised as they yelled fury at him.

If anything, Max's grip on his hammer eased and his shoulders relaxed. He slowly shook his head at his approaching attackers and lowered his weapon.

The diseased slammed into them from all sides, hitting them hard and piling on top of them as they went down. Snarls drowned out the screams. Blood sprayed away from the palace's escapees.

"What were they thinking?" Hawk said.

William shook his head at the stocky boy. "They must have thought they could move through the diseased like Max."

"Why?"

"I'm not sure that's the right question."

"What is, then?"

After taking down a diseased and stealing their top, Max jogged towards the asylum. William tapped the tiles beneath him with his toe. "How many more of them are below us right now? At least the diseased are predictable, and there's no chance of them climbing up onto the roof. What if we're outnumbered by survivors too?"

Hawk stood as dumbstruck as Olga, his mouth slightly open as if the thought of a reply lay on his tongue. William nodded back at the scrunched-up shirt he'd left behind. "Are you going to wear that top?"

Hawk shook his head.

Retrieving Max's shirt, William sat down next to Matilda. Even in the short time they'd been awake, she seemed to have turned paler. Her skin a light shade of green, the sun hit her sweating face like it hit the dew-soaked grass. Holding the shirt up and then turning it around to show her the back, he said, "I'm going to wrap this around your leg. It's cleaner than that other bandage."

While biting on her bottom lip, Matilda breathed through her nose as if even the thought of dressing her wound caused her pain.

William's hands shook as he swaddled her thigh. What if they couldn't find an ointment to deal with the infection?

CHAPTER 2

How many more survivors were there in the palace? And how many watched Max now as he ran towards the asylum? The large grey stone building dominated the landscape. He'd not heard the tone for long, but what he'd give to have it in the background now. The repeated *barp* calling the diseased to the front of the ugly institution. Dragging them away from him and, more importantly, away from the people he intended to liberate from the imposing prison.

The meadow packed with the vile things, their reek so strong it damn near clogged his nostrils. Max slammed into one after the other, sending several of them sprawling as he shoulder-barged his way through. They might have shrieked and cried, the *clack* of their snapping teeth as they chewed at the air around them, but they had no interest in attacking him.

Sometimes their growls and howls sounded like they called his name. *Max. Mad Max.* But they didn't. Of course they didn't. They couldn't speak, so how could they be calling to him?

Vinegar, rot, the glistening film of pus covering their

septic wounds. Loose jaws, long and greasy hair, they surveyed their surroundings, hatred twisting their faces. These creatures had two modes. Rage and torment. Neither were directed at him.

Mad Max. Or were they?

The ground uneven, Max stumbled as he ran. The need to turn around pulled on him, but what good would it do? He'd left Olga behind again. Left her back there with *him*. Maybe they didn't feel anything for one another. But should they really trust Hawk? After what he'd done to them when they were out hunting. But he had saved their lives in the funnel. Had Max gotten him wrong?

Mad Max. Max shook his head to try to banish the imagined calls.

The *clack* of teeth snapped close to him, and Max pulled away, stumbling from his sudden movement. Not that they were trying to attack him. They never tried to attack him.

A once woman shrieked when Max slammed into her, sending her spinning away as she fell on her arse. She searched for prey through her crimson glaze but clearly saw nothing. Blind to anything but the uninfected, she yowled and got to her feet again on wobbly and atrophied legs.

The asylum had no windows. The stone structure standing as imposing as the funnel. Of course he didn't want to go in there, but what else could he do? Say no? Leave innocent women and children inside? They were cold, alone, and no doubt losing their minds. And even if they conquered all of that, at some point they would starve to death.

Mad Max.

His shoulders on fire, each connection with another diseased aggravating the pain in his bones, Max bit down against the sensation and pushed on.

If only he'd spoken to Olga in the night. They'd sat

together for hours. They'd watched the sun set and rise again. He should have swallowed his pride. He should have told her he understood. He could have accepted responsibility for not speaking to her when they were in Umbriel. For not explaining why he'd kept her at arm's length. But instead he sulked. He spent the entire night thinking about himself. About how she'd done him wrong. And now he'd gone again. Left her with Hawk again. And who could blame her for giving up on him? He'd given her no reason to persevere.

His breathing heavy, his legs leaden, his heart sinking, Max reached the entrance to the ornate tunnel. Sweat ran into his sore eyes, and the diseased bumped into him. They were too numerous to avoid.

Mad Max.

Max's hands shook as he flicked through the keys he'd taken from Hawk. Many of them were too small for the lock in front of him. The first one that looked like it might have worked didn't fit. His feet planted on the soft ground, he held onto the cold bars of the tunnel's entrance to prevent himself from getting swept up in the tide of bodies. The creatures nudged him. Bit at the air around him. Moaned as they passed him.

Mad Max.

Clack. The lock finally freed. The hinges groaned and Max barged the diseased aside, kicking several away while he slipped into the tunnel.

Seven diseased followed Max through before he locked the tunnel behind him. He put the keys in his pocket, filled his lungs, the air curdled with diseased funk, and went to work.

Crunch! The first attack sank into the head of a teenage girl. He caved in her skull, forcing her eye from its socket.

Mad Max.

At least Max had the space to work now he'd locked the tunnel.

With all of the diseased down, Max took a moment. Olga stood on the palace's roof, Hawk beside her, as topless as when Max had left him. What a prick. Who was he trying to impress by walking around like that? But Olga was the one who mattered. The desire to wave stirred through the fingers of his right hand. What good would it do? He'd ignored her all evening, and now he was going to wave?

Max walked towards the large steel door at the end of the filigreed tunnel. The tall building blocked the rising sun. There were tens, maybe hundreds of innocent women and children inside. Whatever else happened, they needed to be liberated, and he had to do it. His immunity was equal part curse and gift. He had to use it for good.

His trousers soaked from the morning dew, his legs ached with the exhaustion of the last few weeks. Although, reluctance tugged on his forward momentum more than his fatigue. One of the least inviting places he'd ever seen. Maybe he could go back to Olga before he went in. Explain a few things. Clear the air. Enter the hellish building with a lighter heart.

The diseased all around him. Many of them leaned against the steel tunnel, forced against the filigreed walls by the crush of their peers. Some faces turned his way, although they paid him little mind. Why would they?

Mad Max.

But if he went back to Olga now, he'd have to cross through this lot again. To rub shoulders with the reeking mess of creatures. To inhale their palpable stench.

Mad Max. It took all Max had to not look for the diseased calling to him. It was all in his head. It was all in his head.

Now he'd gotten to the asylum, Max needed to get the

innocent people out. Olga would be there when he'd finished.

Mad Max.

"Shut up!" Max said it beneath his breath. The diseased weren't speaking to him, no matter how many times he imagined it.

Mad Max. The diseased spoke in the voices of his four brothers. The crimson-eyed versions of his brothers. The brothers he'd killed when he found them in Edin.

"Shut up!"

Maaaaaad Max. A long and drawn-out call. The words stretched with their groans and moans.

Mad Max.

Maaaad Max.

No matter how many times he'd heard it, it grated. It turned tension through his shoulders. It tied knots in his guts.

Mad Max.

Nothing but his imagination. He just had to deal with it. "It's not real."

Hey, Max!

That one caught him off guard and Max turned to his right. "Sam?"

"No." He shook his head, a gormless diseased staring back at him. Not Sam. How could it be Sam? Sam had probably turned into a rotting corpse by now. He probably remained in the doorway of their old house, as dead as when Max had left him.

Mad Max. Mad Max.

"What would you have done in my situation?" Unable to find the diseased talking to him, Max turned full circle. "I did the only thing I could. I stopped your suffering. You think that was easy for me?"

Maaaaaaad Max.

"It's not real," Max said. "It's not real." A few feet from the asylum's entrance, Max dug his nail into the large key ring he'd taken from Hawk. He freed the key that opened the filigreed tunnel.

Mad Max.

The ground was soft from all the rain they'd had over the past few weeks. It made it easy enough for Max to force the key into the ground. A cluster of four black steel leaves in the tunnel directly above it. He counted his steps to the large asylum door.

Seven steps. Better to hide it. If he lost the key ring for some reason, he could still get out. And maybe more importantly, he could prevent anyone else from letting the diseased in. He'd seen too many places fall. He couldn't risk giving anyone a chance to leave the gate open.

Mad Max.

"Shut up!"

It took several attempts to find the correct key, but when he finally did, Max opened the large steel door with a *clack*. The sharp note called away into the vast building. The hinges protested against their opening, and Max remained where he stood as he shoved the door wide. This was his last chance to change his mind. Olga remained on the palace's roof. The semi-naked Hawk remained beside her. Did he really want to leave them together? But did he really want to cross through the crowds of diseased again?

Mad Max. Mad Max.

If anything, the calls grew louder. The reminder of what he'd done. Of how he'd left his brothers for dead. Of the violent deaths of many diseased at his hands. What if he'd tried to help them instead? To cure them? No, that would be ridiculous. He wasn't a scientist. He didn't have the skills to help anyone. Not like that at least. But he could help now.

CHAPTER 3

William stood with the others. He bore Matilda's weight where her left leg couldn't. Every few seconds, she winced as if her pain ran through her in pulsating waves, each time catching her unawares.

"I bet it's awful in there," Cyrus said as he watched Max enter the asylum and close the door behind him.

Olga swiped her hair away from her face and held it on top of her head. "I wish I could go in there with him. That place is hell on earth."

"Maybe I shouldn't be saying this," Cyrus said, "but I'm more worried about Max than anyone. The fall of Edin didn't do him any favours."

"It wasn't paradise for us either, you know?" William said.

"Of course." Cyrus dipped a nod. "But Max talked to me a lot on the journey over here. When he couldn't sleep at night, we'd chat. He told me about what he had to do to his family in Edin." The skin around the sides of Cyrus' eyes tightened. A sea of diseased separated them and the giant industrial mess of a building.

Artan put a hand on Cyrus' back. "And?"

"Huh?"

"What did Max say?"

"Oh," a shake of his head, Cyrus said, "he told me that every time he kills a diseased, he sees one of his family. He hears their voices as he's cracking skulls. Even though they're diseased, the sheer violence of it is taking its toll. His role in our group is to slay twenty to fifty times more than any of us ever will. And, really, how different are the diseased from us? Their skulls crack like ours. They bleed like us. Like his family did."

A slight yelp beside him, William tried to catch Matilda's weight, but she insisted she sit by tugging against him.

William hunched down, removed her hummingbird clip, swiped her hair away from her sweating face, and clipped it back again. Bile lifted in his throat to see Hawk had watched him the entire time. "We've gotten this all wrong. Why the hell have we sent Max, our most valuable asset, after a stranger when Matilda needs his help?"

"Dianna's not a stranger," Hawk said.

"She is to us."

"You knew her from Umbriel. She's a good person. She doesn't deserve to be inside that place."

"And Matilda deserves what's happening to her?" After pausing for a moment, his heart pounding, William said, "Look, I'm sure she's wonderful, and maybe there is a need for us to get her out of there, but Matilda's needs are greater. It's messed up that we've put what you want ahead of what Matilda needs. We should have thought about it more. After all, you were prepared to hand us over to Magma. If you'd had your way, we wouldn't even be here. And the very thing that saved us, we've allowed you to use to your advantage."

"I can't change the past."

"And I can't forget it," William said. "If I could go back

now, I'd sneak into your room in Umbriel and cut your throat while you slept."

Hawk's hand went to the scars around his neck, his thick fingers tracing the rope burn and the slashes that ran down his chest.

"I'm not sure this is getting us anywhere," Olga said. "Besides, what could Max have done for Matilda?"

William kept his attention on Hawk. "Don't you dare look at her like that."

Hawk stepped back a pace. "Huh?"

"Don't look at Matilda like you pity her. You could have told us what they had planned for her and Olga when we were in Umbriel. Had you done that, she wouldn't be here in the first place, so save your faux sympathy, yeah?" He turned from Hawk and said to Olga, "Max could have searched the palace to see if they had anything in there we could use. It all happened too quickly. He let his pride get in the way after what happened between you and Hawk, and he rushed off before we could come up with a better plan. What good will Dianna be to us when she and Hawk leave?"

The muscles in the sides of Hawk's jaw tensed and relaxed as he clenched it and stared out over the wasteland.

"And what will he be able to do in that place in the dark? It's huge. And if he can't see where he's going, he'll be in there for hours."

"Dianna—" Matilda paused and dragged in a breath through her clenched teeth. More sweat glistened on her brow "—deserves to be rescued. It's awful in there. She was kind to us. She's the reason we got away. If it wasn't for her, there's no chance we would have toppled this place."

If Hawk felt smug about Matilda backing him up, it didn't show. "So what are your plans?" William said.

"Huh?"

"When Max brings Dianna back to you. What are your plans?"

"If you'll have us, we'll stay with you. Help. Find a way to fix Matilda."

"But after that. Let's say everything works out. What do you have planned then? What's the bigger picture?"

"I've not thought about it." Hawk shrugged. "I dunno. Dianna is my priority and then, uh—" he shrugged again "—go south maybe."

"South of the wall?" Olga said.

"If we can get across. If that's what you all want to do? We'd like to help you if we can. We're stronger together, right?"

"You think Max will want you with us?" Artan said. Not an accusation, a gentle question that needed to be considered if they were planning their future.

Before Hawk could answer, Olga said, "Dianna's a good kid. Like Matilda said, she helped us a lot. She told us about the electricity so we could get the power off."

"Electricity?" Hawk said. "You turned the power off?"

"We smashed the solar panels," Olga said.

Hawk shook his head. "That shouldn't be enough to kill the power on its own."

"There was a metal box. When we opened it up, it was filled with cubes that had wires running from them."

"Batteries," Hawk said.

"If you say so."

"The solar panels gather the sun's rays and convert them into electricity. The batteries store the electricity. They're what powers the place."

"Forgive me," Olga said, "but what are you saying?"

"If we can reconnect the batteries, we might be able to get the power back on to help Max. Can you show me where they are?"

The slightest hint of a smile lifted one side of Olga's mouth. She nodded. "Yes, I can. Let's go."

"I'm going with you," William said. Then to Matilda, "If that's okay?"

Matilda nodded. "You staying here, as much as I love the company, isn't making my leg get any better. You go, see if you can help. In fact"—she winced as she stood up, hopping on her one good leg—"I'm going to come with you."

William flicked his head towards Hawk. "And someone needs to keep an eye on him."

"I am here, you know?" Hawk said.

"I know. Artan, Cyrus, I think you should both come too. If Hawk's telling the truth, we need to get the power back on as soon as possible. The sooner we do that, the sooner we'll be able to find a way to help Matilda."

CHAPTER 4

"That's it, Max, one step at a time, mate. One foot in front of the other. That's all you need to do." It helped to talk to himself. The darkness of the asylum pushed in on him from all sides, amplifying his solitude. He needed the company, and now the diseased had stopped talking to him, he didn't want to let them back in.

Max held the front door key in a pinch, his war hammer in the other hand. Like with the one to lock the ornate tunnel, he'd liberated it from the key ring. Best to keep it separate from the others. The rest of the keys back in his pocket, he reached out for the cold wall on his left side. The large stones were damp and gritty, but he found nowhere to hide the key. If things went south, he needed to be the one who had the control over who left this place.

Several clumsy steps forward, every one spiking his pulse as it threatened to throw him to the ground, Max moved deeper into the pitch-black building and used the wall to guide him. The darkness so complete, it seemed to leech the light from his eyes. It sucked away even the memory of being able to see.

"Ow!" A sharp splinter jabbed into the index finger on Max's right hand. He sucked the tip, felt for the small needle of wood with his tongue, gripped the end with his front teeth, and pulled it out.

The splinter a part of a wooden door, Max knocked and said, "Hello?"

His echo replied.

He shoved the door and it fell open with the groan of old steel hinges. "I'm guessing it's empty, then."

By tapping his foot against the wall and then the wooden door frame, Max felt his way into the cell. The entire place reeked of damp, but a musty funk hung in the air. Stagnation. Dirt. Was someone in there with him? "Hello?"

If they were, they hid it well.

A sharp burn bit into the front of Max's shin from where he'd walked into what must have been a bed for the prisoner. His heart beat in his throat as he reached down and patted the large wooden shelf. Thankfully no one lay there.

Squatting down, Max reached under the bed. A baton ran along the bottom that had a small lip large enough for him to hide the key. He pressed it into place and stood back up again. Whatever else happened, he'd be in charge of who got out.

Both hands on the cold and damp wall, Max's shin still throbbing, and fearful of the uneven floor tripping him, he placed tentative steps one in front of the other. His hushed tones the only company he had in the dark space, he stepped back out into the hallway and said, "Well done, Max. Keep it—"

The scream took flight like the demented cawing of an injured crow. It came from somewhere deep in the building. From within the bowels of the dark and hellish place. Not a cry for help. It came in shrieking waves. The torment of a fractured mind. The ragged panting of insanity. Of someone desperate to escape their thoughts. Of—

Mad Max.

His heart quickened and Max matched his rapid pulse with faster steps as if he could march away from the madness. "That's it, mate, you can do this. Just keep going. One step at a time. One foot in front of the other. Everything's—"

Another shrill cry. Another torn throat. A woman somewhere miles away, but she'd find him. They'd all find him in the darkness. They knew this place better than him. They'd hunt him down. Unless his own mind got to him first.

Mad—

A flash of white light. Max rubbed his stinging forehead from where he'd walked straight into a wall. Grit from the stones mixed with the sweat on his brow. The asylum as dark as ever, his steps crunched over the dirty ground.

But at least there were no diseased in here. No voices of his dead family. They'd moved aside for a greater insanity. While dark, cold, damp, and stinking, at least in here, Max could be free. Much better to deal with the madness of others than his own subsiding mind.

"Now to find Dianna." How many floors did this place have? How many cells? How would he find her? Would he get any sense from the inmates if he asked for directions?

Maybe if he spent longer, he'd come up with a better plan. But as much as this place provided respite from the outside, the insidious insanity would spread through him like an infection. It would occupy him like the damp in every pore of this building, and it would drive his mind away. He tried to call out, but his throat locked.

On his second attempt, he managed it. Weak and strangled, but at least he'd gotten it out. "Dianna?" Jumping at the sound of his own voice, he tracked it as it ran off into the building, finding forks and twists and turns, swimming through the dark and labyrinthine corridors.

"Dianna?" Louder this time.

Another scream answered him. A hyena's cackle. And then sobbing. Hard and uncontrolled. Something primal. Deep, as if it came from the very core of humanity. Suffering since the beginning of time. Loss.

"Just one step at a time," Max told himself. The muscles in his legs were tense with reluctance, but he moved on, tentative in where he put his feet, the darkness holding a million possibilities that could throw him on his arse. While nodding to himself, he repeated, "One step at a time."

Another wooden door on his right, Max snapped his hand away before he felt the sting of another splinter. More people cried from deep within the building. Some of them banged. Tormented animals desperate to be free of this lunatic zoo, they threw hammering blows against doors far, far away. How the hell would he find Dianna in this mess?

As quickly as it had swelled through the place, the insane chorus ended as if the broken residents were of one fractured mind. The silence pressed in on him like a vacuum.

Max found a small window in the cell door. It had three vertical metal bars, each one no more than a foot long. They were about an inch thick and coated with rust. A whisper, no more, he said, "Hello?"

His echo mocked him.

A step closer and he smelled the reek of dirt, damp, and human waste. Old and stale. The memory of a resident long departed. Still, he tried again, and still the asylum held its collective breath. "Hello?"

The swelling of his own pulse throbbed through his ears. Max's forehead touched one of the rusting bars. No matter how many times he blinked, the darkness gave him nothing.

A small shift. The slightest movement inside. A mouse? A rat? Something. "Uh …" Max said. "Hello?"

Slam! The face of a woman hit the other side of the bars.

Max stumbled back several paces, the heel of his right foot catching on the uneven ground. He landed on his arse, the jolt running from his coccyx to the base of his neck. He dropped his hammer with a *clang!*

While the woman laughed, Max pressed his hand to his chest, his heart hammering as he panted to ride out the panic. He felt the cold floor for his weapon.

Slathering, gasping, and grunting. A feral dog both hungry and horny, the woman laughed again. Tittering and shrill, she parroted him. "Hello. Hello. Hello."

Max pushed himself to his feet with shaking arms, his hammer at his side as he stepped closer. "Uh—"

"Uh!" she said. "Uh."

A voice in a cell farther down mimicked her. "Uh."

Then several more. "Uh."

Like strange birds inhabiting a cursed tree, they copied Max.

"Uh."

"Uh."

"Uh."

Mad Max. He batted his forehead with the heel of his right hand. He hit it hard enough to jolt the sound of his family from his mind.

"Uh."

"Uh."

"I'm looking for Dianna!" Max shouted so loud his throat hurt, and the place fell silent again.

"Di—" the woman in front of him said.

Another voice finished for her. "Anna."

"Dianna."

"Dianna."

Max balled his fists and stamped his foot. "Do you know where she is or not?"

The woman's sounds grew into unintelligible caws and cries. She fizzed like an angry cat and hissed like a volatile snake. Get the hell away now or she'd bite. She didn't even know her own self, how the hell would she know Dianna?

When the woman lost control and broke into laughter, Max moved off. This time he used the wall on his right to be as far away from her as possible. Maybe he'd made the wrong choice coming into this place. Maybe he should turn around now and get the hell out of there. Even the diseased with his brothers' voices were better than this. What the hell had he let himself in for?

But what about Dianna? If she still had her mind, he needed to get her out before she lost it. And what about the other prisoners? There were many shrill voices like cackling caged monkeys, but did they represent the majority? As Max tuned into the chorus of chaos, he picked out some of the quieter instruments adding to the symphony. The smaller voices. The weeping children. The gasping women asking for help. No matter what he felt, he had to get them out. There might not be hope for the most vocal in this place, but there were many who could still be saved.

"One foot in front of the other, Max. One step at a time. You can do this." But could he? Every step heavier than the last. Which would be the final one? The breaking of his resolve. Even with children needing to be saved, he had his limits.

CHAPTER 5

William walked on Matilda's left and Artan on her right. She had an arm wrapped around each of them, and each of them held one of her legs, carrying her in a sitting position so she didn't have to walk. Jezebel down the back of his shirt, the large axe head kept tapping the back of William's skull.

The pitched roof had been built for drainage. Not only did they have to walk at a slant, but the chunky ceramic tiles made for uneven footing. Every time William pulled Matilda's leg too high, she winced. The shirt Max had given to Hawk, which he'd wrapped around her thigh, glistened with blood. "I'm so sorry," he said.

A shake of her head, Matilda said, "You're doing your best. It's fine."

Olga walked ahead of them, leading the way. Only she and Matilda had been to the courtyard before. She had Cyrus and Hawk flanking her.

"Just put me down here," Matilda said. They were close enough to see the courtyard.

Artan said, "You sure?"

"The less I move, the better."

And the less William and Artan moved her, the better. Especially William. At least she had the good grace to keep that thought to herself.

After setting Matilda on the tiles, William crouched down and stroked her hair away from her sweating face, tucking it behind her ear. "Are you okay?"

"As okay as I can be."

"The second we get the power back on, I promise we'll get into the palace and find something to help with your infection."

Although she nodded and tried to smile, her fear remained in her deep brown eyes. The longer it took, the worse it would be for her. Before William could promise her again, she reached up and held the side of his face. "You're doing everything you can. That's what matters most." She leaned forwards and kissed him, her lips dry against his.

After they'd separated, William had the salty taste of her sweat on his lips.

There were at least one hundred black panels in the large courtyard. Uniform in size, each one about six feet long and four feet wide. All of them were tilted at an angle of roughly forty-five degrees. There were about twenty rows of five in the rectangular courtyard. Before it had been taken over as the host for the panels, it would have been a pleasant place to spend a sunny afternoon. Sheltered from the wind, it had the remains of what looked like a fountain in its centre.

Surrounded by Grandfather Jacks' palace on all sides, the courtyard had windows looking into it. Scores of diseased meandered through the panels, and there were many more in the palace. An open doorway at the far end allowed the free movement of the creatures between the palace and the courtyard. A gate hung open that, when closed, would prevent the diseased's movement.

Every panel had been damaged, cracks running across them, shards of the shattered tiles embedded in the broken glass. There were holes by William's feet from where the tiles had been torn from the roof. Now he'd put down Matilda, he held Jezebel in one hand while reaching down to wriggle a tile free with the other. As he lifted it clear, it caught the steel guardrail around the edge of the roof with a *ching!* A diseased nearby snapped its head in his direction, staring at him as it snarled, its top lip raised, its jaw slack.

A tight grip on the rough tile, William wound it back and launched it like he would a Frisbee. It spun, the corner connecting with the eye socket of the creature, knocking it down. The thing wailed as it lay on its back and threw its limbs around like a spider having a seizure. When it scrambled to its feet again, it had a deep cut in its right cheek that revealed the white of its skull in the glistening wound.

Cyrus snorted a laugh, liberated a tile like William had, and launched it into the foetid crowd. The first time he'd been able to attack the diseased without shitting himself. Maybe he should be allowed this luxury.

Before Cyrus could pull another tile free, Hawk, who'd walked all the way around the courtyard to inspect it, said, "The panels will be fine for now."

"For now?" William said.

"They'll still generate power, but after it's rained a few times, the water will get in the cracks and ruin them."

"But we'll be long gone by then, right?" Cyrus said.

Hawk looked over the courtyard and shrugged. "Here's hoping."

"Okay," William said, walking to the edge of the roof, "let's do this."

"Y-you've seen how many diseased are down there, right?" Cyrus said.

"Have you seen the state of Matilda? Regardless of how

many diseased are down there, she needs help soon. Every second spent here is time taken away from finding something that will make her feel better."

"Where do you expect to find something to make her feel better?" Hawk said. He only held William's eye for the briefest of moments before he looked away like he knew something.

"There has to be something in the palace, right? Grandfather Jacks lived here for long enough. They must have some medicine of some sort."

"First, we have to find a way to clear the diseased out of the courtyard," Hawk said.

"*All* of them?" William said. "That could take hours. And what about Max? What will he manage to achieve in the pitch black of the asylum? We need to get down there and get the power back on as soon as possible." He walked along the edge of the courtyard until he came to the metal box at the back. It had cubes inside like Olga had described, wires lying on the stone ground beside them from where she'd torn them free. "Those are the batteries, right? And we need to get down there and reconnect them?"

"That is what we need to do," Hawk said, "but you need to slow down."

Maybe he imagined it, but when William looked across at Matilda, she'd already turned several shades paler. The morning sun glistened on her skin. "If I slow down too much, she'll die."

"Let's take a vote." Hawk raised his right hand in the air. "All of those who want to at least formulate a plan before we go into that courtyard, raise your hand."

Everyone but Artan and William raised their hands.

"And all of those who want to save Matilda's life raise your hand," William said.

They all raised their hands.

Olga this time. "Hawk's right. We can't save Matilda if we kill ourselves in that courtyard. Remember, I've been down there once already."

It had been easier to argue with Hawk, but when the same message came from Olga, William had to admit it made sense. Like him, she had Matilda's best interests at heart.

Turning his back on the courtyard, William spun Jezebel in his grip. Perfectly balanced, it twirled in his hands, begging to be used. He halted the swing by snapping his hands tight on the handle and turned on Olga. "So what do you suggest? How long do we wait?"

Olga shrugged. "We need to find a way to get them out of the courtyard."

"Hardly a plan though, is it?"

"When we needed to disconnect the batteries, Matilda hung down into the courtyard to drag the diseased over, which allowed me to get down there."

Another wince broke Matilda's stoic expression, her face turning puce with her clear pain. "But if we do that," William said, "it will bring more diseased into the courtyard from the palace. We could end up with ten times the number of diseased down there. Was that gate open before?"

Olga shook her head. "No, it was locked. We had to open it to spread the disease through the palace."

"What was it locked with?"

"A padlock."

"We've not got another one of them, have we?"

Olga looked at her feet.

But a peg might do it. When they closed the gate, a tab of steel attached to the wall would poke through the frame. It had a hole in it where the padlock must have been attached. Wedge something in that and it should hold the creatures back. At least for long enough to allow them to work.

The others talked amongst themselves as William walked

to the edge of the courtyard. His toes just inches from the guardrail, several diseased fixed on him, all of them working their mouths as if their jaws ached.

"So now we need to work out how to get them out of the courtyard," Cyrus said.

If they waited to come up with a plan, they'd be waiting all night. If they could lock the gate, it would stop more diseased entering the space. At least they could then take the fight to the creatures who remained in the courtyard.

"It's no good," William said. "We don't have time for this shit." A glance at Matilda. She knew him better than anyone. Maybe she saw his plans. Maybe not.

William reached across to Artan and tore the spear from his back. Jezebel in his other hand, he jumped from the roof to screams from both Matilda and Cyrus. As he fell, he threw the spear, driving it through the eye socket of one of the diseased.

Jezebel in a two-handed grip, he threw several wild throws of the heavy weapon and cleared his immediate vicinity of the damned creatures. But he hadn't moved quickly enough to silence their screams. The diseased inside the palace all turned to him. Surrounded on all sides, they stared through the windows before descending on the doorway between the palace and the courtyard. While the diseased from inside charged at him, those in the courtyard —a hundred of them if not more—zeroed in on his position. The smashed solar panels prevented them from charging in a straight line. Although, the layout of the courtyard only bought him seconds at best.

CHAPTER 6

"It's okay, Max. Everything will be fine. One step at a time. Slow and steady wins the race." Whether clichés or utter nonsense, it didn't matter as long as he filled the silence. The silence invited the voices back in.

Max slammed his right knee into another wall, a sharp sting streaking up his thigh into his groin. He turned right down the next corridor, stumbling blind in the dark labyrinth.

The screams continued throughout the place, some far away, some from the cells right next to him. Some of the inmates tried to talk to him.

"Dianna?" His voice ran ahead of him and died as if smothered by the darkness. "Dianna?"

Too many raised stones on the ground to count, Max stubbed the toe of his boot again and stumbled forwards by several steps, his left arm windmilling, his right hand clinging onto his war hammer.

"Everything's fine." Max's heart raced towards panic, sending pains through his chest. As much as he talked to himself, nothing could prevent the images. They'd been lurking in the corners of his head. They now played out on the projector in his mind. It made no difference whether he opened or closed his eyes because the darkness provided the black screen for the hellish showreel.

Diseased eyes. Red, glistening. Snapping maws, many of them with holes torn in the cheeks, the wounds glossed with the milky pus of infection. His hammer caving in skulls, reshaping the faces of the already twisted creatures. His brothers' faces. *Mad Max*. He saw his family one after the other. They were themselves momentarily before their eyes filled with blood and their jaws fell loose. Their heads also buckled beneath his heavy hammer blows. *Mad Max*.

"Dianna?" The echo in the cavernous hallways threw his desperation back at him. He'd never find her in this place. How could he? He couldn't see anything. Daylight would banish the images, even if he did have to face the diseased outside. But had he gone too far now? How could he find his way out again?

"When I do find her, at least I'll be able to get out of here. Get both of us out of here. Dianna!"

As he'd done in the last few corridors he'd entered, Max felt his way around the bend, using the wall to guide him, to get an understanding of which direction he should walk. He stepped several paces away from the walls. From the cell doors.

And a good job too. Footsteps on his right. Bare feet on the stone floor, they ended with a *crash* as the person in the cell slammed against their locked door.

Several women and children screamed somewhere else in the asylum, and Max's already rapid pulse ran quicker. But he'd given himself enough space. "Nothing to worry about. They can't get to me here."

A snarling and growling from the cell on his right.

"Huh?" Max said. "There are diseased in here?"

The phlegmy note came from deep inside the creature's chest.

"Shut it out, Max." He raised his voice. "Dianna?"

"Dianna!" the woman in the cell beside him said.

"You're not infected?"

The woman on his right repeated, "Dianna."

"Do you know Dianna?" Maybe Max should have been more cautious, but one of them had to know something.

"Know Dianna?" The woman sent it back to him as a question.

Max shook his head and sighed. "Never mind."

"Let me out."

The most human thing she'd said, it halted Max mid step.

"Please," the woman said. "Let me out of here. I've been in here so long. I just want to be free."

"I'm not sure what free is," Max said.

"You'd have a better idea if you'd spent as long in here as I have."

"It's not good outside, you know?"

"It's not good in here."

"There are too many diseased."

"Better diseased than—"

The woman paused as a shrill cry soared through the hallways of the asylum.

"If you let me out, I'll make it worth your while."

The whole place stank, but as he talked to the woman, Max managed to pinpoint her stench, and he ruffled his nose. His stomach turned backflips.

"Please," the woman said, "I'll do whatever you want."

His hands clapped to his ears, Max shook his head. Dirt mixed with the reek of human waste. The damp in the air turned the funk tangible. "I don't *want* you to do anything."

"Come on, big boy. Come closer and let me out."

What harm would it do? The more he let out, the more

people he'd have to help him find Dianna. The less time he'd have to spend inside his own head. They couldn't all be nuts, could they? And those who were would be managed by the group. Also, what about the children? Hell, Dianna was no more than a child herself. If he started letting people out, he'd find her much sooner.

The keys rattled in Max's trembling hands, and he approached the cell door on shaking legs. "This is the right thing to do."

"Huh?" the woman said.

Too many keys to choose from, Max picked one and stabbed it against the wooden door, looking for the response of metal against metal. At least if he found the lock, he could then methodically go through the keys on the ring.

The woman on the other side of the door breathed in ragged waves. Slathering, she panted like an animal, forcing halitosis out into the hallway.

"Do you know where the lock is?" Max said.

"Higher," the woman said.

Tapping the wood along the left side of the door, Max worked his way up.

"Into the middle more."

Tap. Tap. Tap.

Totally blind in the asylum, everything had to be methodical. An inch at a time, he worked towards the hole with the bars in it and closer to the woman.

"More to your right," she said.

At least she could still communicate. She hadn't completely lost her mind.

"Do you know Dianna?" Max said.

"Yes."

"You do?"

"Yes."

"And you can take me to her?"

"It'll be hard in this darkness, but I'm sure I can, yes. Now come more into the middle."

Slow and steady. *Tap. Tap. Tap.*

The woman moved fast, striking like a viper. Max screamed when she reached through the bars and grabbed his wrist. He dropped the keys and they hit the stone floor with a *splash.*

She reached out with her second hand, grabbed his wrist with both, and tugged on his arm. His forehead slammed against the thick wooden door with a *boom,* the connection sending a splash of white light through his mind's eye.

The second tug slammed Max against the door again.

He dropped the war hammer with a clatter and braced against the third pull. But the woman was strong and her grip true. She must have had her foot pressed against the other side of the door because she overpowered him, pulling his arm so the bars were up to his shoulder.

"What do you want?" Max said. "I'm trying to get you out of there. Is that not enough?"

The woman laughed. Several others in the asylum joined in. She screeched, "Dianna," and again gathered a chorus of others as enthralled by the events as her.

When Max felt something soft and warm, he didn't work out what it was until the inmate said, "Have you ever felt a woman like me before?"

As much as he wanted to withdraw, she had him pinned, using his trapped hand to rub her own breasts.

"What does it feel like, sweetie?"

His shoulder on fire with how hard she tugged, Max's voice broke. "What are you doing? I was trying to get you out of there. What the hell are you doing?"

"I want you to come in here. I'm giving you a sample of the goods."

If she pulled any harder, she'd dislocate his shoulder. Tears in his eyes, his voice wavering, Max said, "Let me go!"

The woman's voice deepened and crackled like distant thunder. "This place doesn't let anyone go."

Before she could do permanent damage, Max closed a hard grip around her exposed breast. She screamed and let go.

Withdrawing so quickly he slammed his hand against the bars in the door. The back of it throbbed as if he might have broken something, but Max managed to get free before she grabbed him a second time.

Her arm flapping around like an octopus' tentacle, she desperately tried to grab him, her hand slapping against the wooden door.

Crouched down, Max retrieved his war hammer and then the key ring. The keys back in his pocket, he gripped the handle of his weapon. His hand stinging from where she'd dragged it through, he wound his hammer back. He should shatter her arm. Teach her a lesson.

"I'm going to end you," the woman hissed. "I'm going to get out of here, hunt you down, and gouge your fucking eyes out. You won't fool us. We know you're one of them. One of Grandfather Jacks' lot."

If this woman had the ability to listen to reason, he might have engaged with her.

The spray of spittle hit Max's face when she spat from the cell. The patter of her bare feet ran away from the door. When she came back, quicker than before, Max moved aside at the last minute, narrowly avoiding the contents of her waste bucket. The rancid liquid spewed through the small barred window. The heady reek caught in his throat and he covered his nose with his forearm.

What use was he in here? He couldn't see a damn thing. Many of the people in the cells were quiet and subdued. But

There were plenty of people he could help inside this large dark institution. He could do something about them.

Mad Max.

And hopefully it would stop the voices. A deep inhale and one last glance at Olga. She might have stood next to Hawk, but they had distance between them. If only he'd spoken to her when he'd had the chance. If only he'd learned his lesson the first time. But he'd get back to her after this. He'd make it right.

Max stepped through the doorway of the cold and dark asylum and froze.

Mad Max.

The daylight from outside lit the way for several feet before it was consumed by the shadows. Like with the gate to the tunnel, he couldn't leave this door open. He couldn't let this place fall like Edin had. And what benefit would he get from a few feet of daylight?

Mad Max.

Darkness swamped the place when Max closed the door. Darkness and quiet. Peace. He waited for the call, but it didn't come. The white noise of the diseased banished. The voices of his brothers gone.

Several taps with the metal key against the lock beneath the handle. He finally found the hole, slid the key in, and locked the door.

The wall on his right to guide him, he kept one hand on the damp stone, every step forwards into the unknown. But at least he'd left those things behind. For now, he could forget the echoes from his past and focus on what lay ahead. For many, the asylum meant incarceration and madness. For Max in that moment, it meant sanctuary. But now he had to find Dianna.

how could he trust a single one of them? Especially when they thought he had something to do with Grandfather Jacks.

"I need to get back to the others," Max said, speaking beneath his breath so the woman in the cell didn't hear him. "There has to be another way. This isn't working. I could be in here for days."

The smell from the woman's waste bucket curdled the air, the stench getting stronger with every passing second. Max turned away from her cell and headed back the way he'd come. He needed daylight. Even with the diseased outside. Even with them calling him *Mad Max*. It would give him space to think straight. He needed a better plan than wandering the dark corridors of this hellish place like a lost inmate.

CHAPTER 7

Squelch! William tugged the spear from the dead diseased's eye socket. Jezebel in one hand, the spear in the other. He closed in on the gate and used his foot to drag it across, the large metal frame swinging towards the wall. And he would have shut it in one were it not for the *tonk* of the solid door colliding with a diseased woman's forehead.

The diseased in the courtyard weaved through the solar panels, closing in on him. Several of them screamed as if arguing with one another; as if each one wanted to be the first to tear his throat out.

One eye on those charging across the courtyard, William clenched his jaw and shoved the gate with his foot. The creatures packed the doorway and shoved back.

"They're closing in on you, William."

Like he didn't fucking know. William resisted the urge to look over his shoulder again. Whatever else happened, he had to get the gate shut. The sole of his boot pressed against the gate's frame, he shoved for a second time, the muscles in his thighs burning, his standing foot slipping on the flagstone floor.

One final shove helped William thread the steel tag embedded in the wall through the frame. He slid Artan's spear into the hole in the tag. A wooden peg to prevent the diseased from shoving the gate open, they now gripped the bars of their prison and shook the steel frame. Wails and screams, they bit at the air, their rancid and bloody maws working overtime. But they were contained. For now.

William met the first of the courtyard runners with a full-bodied swing. Jezebel's wide arc ended in a *crunch* from where the head of his axe buried in the bald head of the diseased. He caught the next one on the upswing. A girl, no more than ten, his blow lifted her clean off the ground, her arms windmilling as she flew backwards. She hit the closest solar panel with a crack and slid to the ground.

A diseased on his right, too close for William to swing at, he flinched. But the creature went down. Cyrus whooped and punched the air with a clenched fist before he retrieved another roof tile to throw.

Sweat stung William's eyes, his grip moist against Jezebel's handle. Adrenaline threatened to take away his coordination, his heart hammering.

The diseased weaved through the solar panels like dancers, their hips snaking to accommodate their mazy run. A hundred, maybe more, William yelled and attacked the next one to come close. A large man with long hair and tattoos, his skull might have been bigger than the last few, but it would have to be made from steel to win out against a blow from Jezebel.

Already out of breath, William couldn't keep this up.

Olga screeched as if she'd heard his thoughts. "You need to get the hell out of there, William."

At least he'd closed the gate. He'd done the hardest part.

William shoulder-barged the next diseased aside. A boy

dressed in just a pair of trousers, he bore similar scars to Hawk.

The majority of the pack came from the right, so William went left. He met the next diseased with a kick to the chest, knocking the creature back and jumping its flailing arms as he hurdled it.

No need to look over his shoulder, the yells from the creatures behind told him all he needed to know.

William jumped onto the glass surface of a solar panel, its centre decorated with the burst star of cracked glass. On his first step, the glass crunched beneath his weight. On his second, the panel split diagonally across the centre and slid away, dragging him back towards the diseased.

White light burst through the back of William's head, driven through his vision by a diseased knee, the creature leaping for where he'd been seconds before. It landed on the panel ahead of him and slid like he had.

William stamped on the diseased's head before it could get up. He swept the feet away from the next creature. Although where one or two fell, many replaced them, coming at him from all angles.

Dropping onto his front, William shoved Jezebel beneath a solar panel's metal frame before crawling under after her. He kicked his legs so the clawing hands couldn't grab him, his trousers preventing their long nails from tearing his skin. But a tight grip wrapped around both of William's ankles. The clench so strong it stung. They pulled him back before he could reach his axe.

The rough stone dragged William's shirt up and cut his front. He kicked out again, broke free and spun onto his back. But the diseased grabbed him again and pulled.

William caught the panel's frame just before it went from his reach, his arms burning with the strain. Although the panel blocked his view of the diseased, he saw it when it snapped at thin air, aiming a bite at where his shin had been before he kicked it free.

Snapping his legs under the panel with him, William scrambled onto all fours and crawled out of the other side, retrieving Jezebel as he got to his feet.

His throat dry and his pulse raging, sweat burned William's eyes as the screams closed in on him again. The solar panel had bought him seconds at best.

CHAPTER 8

"I just need to retrace my steps," Max said to himself as he slowly walked in the pitch dark. "One foot in front of the other, go back the way I came in, and everything will be fine. Simple."

The pressing darkness around Max smothered him like a thick and itchy blanket. Getting out would be very far from simple. But what other choice did he have? With no lights, he couldn't do anything effective in this place. The reek of the woman's waste still in his nostrils, the cries of distress and torment the soundtrack to his retreat, he continued his search for the exit.

His breathing heavy, his feet slammed down hard from where he misjudged his steps. The stone floor made for an uneven ground, but not as uneven as he anticipated. His hands out to either side, the war hammer gripped in his right, he walked out of there with exaggerated steps as if he wore clown's shoes.

Ten to fifteen steps later, the murmurings of *Mad Max* at the back of his mind, Max swiped his hands out in front of him. "Where's the wall?" He met thin air. "It should be here."

Another step forward, another slash of thin air. "When I find it—*Mad Max*—I can turn left. But if I can't find it …"

Mad Max.

Violence flashed through his mind: blood, breaking bones, bleeding eyes. Max slammed the heel of his right hand against his forehead. "Get out. This isn't how it works. There aren't any diseased here."

His breathing quickened and his chest tightened.

Mad Max.

"Just calm down, Max." He drew a deep breath, inhaling the damp and stale air. "Stay calm and keep your head. You'll find the way out of here."

Bang!

"Argh!" Max jumped away from the sound on his right.

Someone had slammed against their locked cell door. "Get me out of here," the woman said. "Please, I've done nothing wrong. Please! It's so dark. I'm not sure how much longer I can take this."

"You and me both," Max said.

"You're a guard. How is this anywhere near as bad for you as it is for me?"

"I'm *not* a guard," Max said.

"Sure you're not." The woman's tone turned darker, the edges of her words sharpening, cutting to his core. "You're bound to say that because if we get a hold of you, you're done for."

"I'm not. I—"

Mad Max.

Little point in talking to the woman, Max turned away from her and continued to reach into the blinding darkness. It reminded him of a game he used to play with his brothers. They'd take turns putting on a blindfold and they'd pretend to be one of the diseased. They'd walk around the house with their arms out in front of them, trying to find the others. One time, his brothers put his blindfold on and all of them went out. It took him at least an hour before he gave up and realised he'd been in the house on his own for most of the time. The memory of a smile tickled his lips and he muttered, "Bastards."

The images of childhood were shoved aside by memories of his brothers when he'd last seen them. Of Matthew. When he'd gone back home after being freed from the labs in Edin, Matthew had been the worst of the lot. His left cheek had been torn away. A flap of bloody and fleshy skin as large as Max's palm hung down. It exposed his jaw, showing the skeletal workings of his gnashing teeth. And then when he stabbed him … he winced at the memory of the stench that came from him as if his guts had already rotted. Max gripped tighter on his war hammer as the actions of ending his family ran through him. As he lived it all over again.

Mad Max.

"Just keep walking, Max." He shook his head as if it would discard the memories. But they were seared into his mind. He'd take them to the grave. "Just keep walking." The gnashing teeth worked in his mind. A cross-section of his brother's face, his bones mechanical as they chewed the air.

Mad Max.

"Huh?" Louder this time, Max turned one way and then the other. "Who said that?"

Laughter came from Max's left. It started quietly and grew. First one inmate, and then one in the cell next to her.

Thuds then joined the chorus from where they kicked their cell doors. Not just them, but others too. Maddened horses in stables, they wanted the hell out of there. *Thud. Thud. Thud.*

The thuds stopped, but the laughter endured. It morphed into something else. It ran away with the women, shrill and insane. They'd lost control.

"You'll get out of here, Max." He shook his war hammer and nodded to himself. At least the sounds helped him avoid the doors on either side. They kept him in the centre of the dark corridor. The correct corridor? Who the hell knew? "Better to keep walking than give up," he said. "Get out of here, get back to the others, and get a better plan than this. It's madness to walk through the dark and expect to find Dianna."

"Dianna?" someone on Max's left said.

Even if he had to fight every diseased between the palace and the asylum to clear a path so the others could join him, then so be it. He needed company when he returned to this place.

Mad Max.

The head of Max's war hammer hit the wall first. He reached out to the cold stone. "There shouldn't be a wall here." He turned left, tripping on the uneven floor before stumbling forwards and slamming into a cell door with a *thud!*

An inmate inside screamed. A child's scream. Fear rather than madness. The kid sobbed and muttered one word on repeat. "Mama, Mama, Mama."

Max blinked as if he could will his stinging eyes to see through the darkness. "Mama's not here," he said.

The sobbing child gasped. The crying stopped.

"I need to find a way to get you out of here. To get you *all* out of here. But it's not safe at the moment. I will be back, I promise."

"Every time I speak to a guard, they tell me to wait."

"I'm not a …" But what did it matter? A lump caught in Max's throat. "How long have you been in here?"

"I don't know."

"When did you see your mum last?"

"I don't know. None of us boys have seen our mums in a long time. I wouldn't even recognise her now."

His war hammer in his right hand, Max reached up with his left and pressed his palm against the wooden door. Unlike the front door, it had been locked with a large metal bolt. If he kept the noise down, he could get the kid out of there without disturbing the others. What harm would it do to let a child go free?

While biting down on his bottom lip, Max pulled the small knob on the bolt away from the door, the action gritty with rust. Just as he drew breath to reassure the kid, a woman's voice burst from the cell. "Please let us out."

Max stopped. "H-how many of you are in there?"

"Six. Now please let us out. We won't be any trouble, I promise."

Maybe the kid he'd spoken to, or maybe another one, but the sobbing of a small child stuttered from the darkness. If he let them out, who would they let out in turn? If the cells were only locked with bolts, the place could be overrun in seconds, and if he couldn't see a thing, what could he do about it? What would this place be like if the vocal minority took over? What would happen to him if enough of them thought he worked for Grandfather Jacks?

Max stepped back several paces.

"Please!" the woman said. "We've been in here for weeks. Months even. Please!"

While shaking his head, Max muttered, "It's not safe. It's not safe." And until he found a way out of there, it would be madness to let other people out with him.

More screams from far away. They searched the darkness of the corridors as if they might return to the women who'd released them with some kind of wisdom. A mental ointment for the infection of the mind. An easing of the insanity running laps in their skulls. No way could he let them out with him. Their salvation would come. Of that he'd make sure. Just not yet.

"I'm sorry." Max stepped farther away from the cell he'd nearly opened. "I'm sorry."

Max slammed into another wall. Which way to go now? He turned right. The cries soaring through the place begged him to liberate them, but what good would that be if he couldn't even liberate himself?

His legs weak and wobbly, Max managed several more steps before he sat down on the cold ground, cross-legged. His head in his hands, he blinked in the darkness, his tired eyes burning. "What good am I if I can't even liberate myself?"

CHAPTER 9

The diseased closed in from all sides again, some of them even crawling after William beneath the solar panel. In an open space he might have tried to fight them, but the panels were too close to allow him to work. With his friends at least fifteen feet away on the roof, he had to find a way out of this mess on his own.

The only way to use his weapon, he brought Jezebel over his head in a vertical swing, splitting the skull of a diseased. A woman with black hair, her cranium cracked, her legs turned instantly ineffective, and she crumpled. Her face slammed against the edge of a solar panel.

As another diseased fell across his path, William stamped on its head and broke its skull. A child no more than about eight or nine years old. Naked from the waist up, the boy had scars around his neck. But being a child made him a cinch to kill. At that moment he was fighting the diseased, and the more easily they yielded, the better.

More creatures from the right than any other direction, so William charged left and slammed both hands into the chest of a tall diseased man. The large body drove the others behind him back. William darted past him and leaped onto another solar panel.

He'd jumped without looking. Jezebel made it hard to be nimble, but the crumbling glass sheet over the solar panel made it impossible. The glass had turned to dust in some places, shingle in others. Like running up a mirror covered in sand, his feet slipped away from him, and he slammed down onto the panel with both knees before he slid back down.

This time William spun, turning his momentum into an attack. He buried Jezebel into the arm of a diseased, the creature yelling, blood belching from the deep wound.

Another diseased tried to grab William and he ducked, but one caught him from behind. It pulled him so close its rancid breath smothered him. Its teeth snapped with a sharp *clack* next to his right ear.

William slammed the end of Jezebel's handle into the beast's soft body. It forced another wave of rancid breath from it with a gasp, but it let go. Three more blows with the wooden handle sent three more diseased stumbling back. He caught a flash of Matilda standing among the others on the roof. Her left foot pointed in a tiptoe from where she tried to take the pressure off her thigh. As pale as when he'd left her, she chewed on her bottom lip. An uninjured Matilda would have been beside him by now. But in this, he was on his own.

The blunt end of Jezebel as effective as the axe head, William kept away the diseased closest to him. Another gap opened and he made a mazy retreat, the panels working in his favour, the route after him much harder to follow because of their layout.

A hiss in his left ear, William pulled aside at the last moment. Closer than the previous one, the creature still caught air with the snapping *clack* of its biting jaw.

They were too close. There were too many. He couldn't see a path out of there.

Movement flashed to William's right. Someone hopped across the tops of the solar panels. They moved one step at a time like when Matilda had crossed the logs in the national service area. Olga reached the panel closest to William and slid down its forty-five-degree slope. She led with the point of her sword, spearing a fat diseased woman through the face, pulling it out with a spray of blood as the woman fell away.

The mob around William turned one way and then the other. It gave him enough time to act. He drove Jezebel's curved blade into the neck of a woman close to him while Olga went to work, her right arm moving like a piston as she speared face after face.

A gap opened between them. William crossed it and pressed his back to Olga's. Gasping, he said, "Thanks."

"Don't thank me yet."

While he drove vertical axe swings, she continued to stab the diseased. Both of them effective enough in their own way, but they were still outnumbered. They could only keep this up for so long.

"William!" Artan waved before jumping down into the courtyard, a spear in one hand, his knife in the other.

The panels hid him from sight, but it gave them something to head towards. Hawk jumped down after Artan.

Were it not for the narrow channels between the solar panels, they would have been dead by now. It forced the diseased into a funnel. At every crossroads, Olga threw a flurry of stabs. It bought them enough time to cross to the next narrow path.

Sweat stung William's eyes as he worked. He drove some of the diseased back with blows to the head. With others he used the flat end of the thick metal blade. As blunt as a hammer and as heavy, it did almost as much damage as the sharpened edge.

Matilda and Cyrus remained on the roof, launching tiles into the diseased.

Olga and William burst through the final gap between the solar panels and into the space Hawk and Artan had cleared for them. They both glistened with sweat. They both moved like machines, killing diseased after diseased.

A second to catch his breath behind the safety of Artan and Hawk, William pulled one of the spears from the sheath on Hawk's back. William held it up at Cyrus, who stared at it for a second.

"Come down here. We need your help."

"But—"

"Now!" As he said it, William jabbed the spear in Cyrus' direction.

The boy's bottom lip buckled, but he jumped down and took the weapon.

Olga had joined the boys' attack on the diseased. They'd already formed a protective semicircle, the gated entrance and batteries within their control.

"Use the spear to stab the diseased in the palace," William said. "You have the gate to protect you, but you need to make sure they don't keep pushing against it. I'm worried the wooden shaft won't hold."

Although Cyrus looked like he might argue, he clearly thought better of it, turning to the gate while William forced his way next to his three fighting friends.

The bodies were mounting up and they lay on the stone ground like sandbags. The diseased charged, many of them tripping over their fallen brethren. Before they'd regained their balance, they met the sharp tip of a spear, sword, or the razor's edge of an axe.

"Get to work on the batteries," William called to Hawk.

It took a second, but Hawk pulled away from the fight and hunched down in front of the metal box. The sooner they got the power back on, the sooner they could get out of this hellish courtyard.

William couldn't hear anything over the sound of his own ragged breaths. His arms were aching with fatigue. Wielding the heavy Jezebel felt like trying to fight with a battering ram, but he found the strength he needed for every swing. No wonder Magma had arms as thick as William's thighs.

If Olga and Artan suffered like William, they hid it well. The pair of them danced like they were born for this. Olga a wild and frenzied mess of bloody fury; Artan an artist with calm and poise. One as deadly as the other.

And like that, the diseased were defeated. Blood coated the stone ground. The bodies lay piled one on top of the other. A sea of diseased corpses. "Jeez," William said with an exhale, wiping his sweating brow with his forearm, "I didn't think they'd ever run out."

Both Artan and Olga remained alert, scanning left and right.

Hawk remained crouched over the batteries when Cyrus said, "Guys! A little help over here!"

The spear William had used as a pin had snapped. It lay in pieces on the ground.

Artan shot past William and grabbed a length of wire from next to the batteries.

Diseased faces pressed against the bars of the gate. The sheer weight of bodies forced it open by a few inches. Cyrus stabbed them and shoved it closed again.

Artan threaded the cable through the hole. He pressed his own boot against the gate to help Cyrus and tied a quick knot before pulling it tight with both hands.

The gate held.

Olga came to Artan's side with several more short pieces

of wire. She handed them to Artan one after the other. He used each one to tie the gate in place, every knot tighter than the one before.

All the while, Hawk worked on the batteries, frowning into the large box.

Artan and Olga smiled at one another, a nod of recognition passing between the two before they turned away from the gate. "That should hold it," Artan said.

The diseased inside the palace as loud as ever, but the fallen in the courtyard gave the enclosed space a sense of calm by comparison. Now they needed to wait for Hawk to finish.

"Artan!" Cyrus yelled.

William's settling heart took flight again, and he clapped his hand to his chest.

It took for Cyrus to launch his spear for William to see the cause of his concern. A diseased woman, no taller than Olga and, from the twist of her vicious face, no less fierce.

Cyrus' launched spear missed and clattered into a solar panel beside her before falling to the ground.

Unlike the other diseased, this one jumped the fallen, landing inside the semicircle of protection the diseased corpses had upheld for them.

A large tile spun over William's head and struck the woman in the centre of her face. The corner dented her cheek and she fell backwards.

Cyrus shoved William aside. Weaponless, he stood over the woman and stamped on her head. Once, twice, three times, the woman's nose turned into mush, her mouth still working as she chewed on the air.

Crunch! The woman's head gave and she fell limp.

Cyrus panted like the rest of them and turned to Hawk. "How much longer before the power's back?"

"Nearly there," Hawk said.

William couldn't help but smile. "You know," he said to Cyrus, "maybe there is a warrior in you."

Cyrus' stoic expression softened. "I'm just doing what needs to be done."

CHAPTER 10

Mad Max.

It wouldn't leave him. His war hammer in one hand, his forehead in the other, Max leaned forwards. Were it not so dark, he would have been staring at the cold stone floor that turned his bottom numb, but he couldn't see an inch in front of his face, let alone a foot or more. No matter how he rocked from side to side, he found no comfort on the frigid ground.

And what about the kid he'd left in the cell? How many of them were there in this place? And how could he walk away from them? But if he opened the doors to any of these cells and they didn't have Dianna in, what would he be inviting out into the corridors? At the moment he had—

Mad Max.

He had control. Control of the asylum even if he didn't have control of his own mind. He didn't need screaming insanity running through the corridors with him. "But …" he said to himself, his voice searching the darkness before dying somewhere in the abyss, "what if I let out enough people for them to show me a way out of here? What if I let out enough people for one of them to be Dianna so I won't have to come back again?"

But if he let everyone out and they found the exit, he'd have to give them the key. For their own safety, he couldn't let them outside with the diseased. Every one of them would be turned, including Dianna.

Caws, shrieks, and cries searched the corridors as if they might get an answer. Some way to placate their insanity. But it would never come.

"Right, Max." He pushed off against the cold and gritty ground and got to his feet. "One thing you know for sure is you won't be getting out of here by sitting on your arse all day. That's a fact."

So much adrenaline had coursed through his system it had left him weak. Shaking legs, a heavy heart and deep aches in his bones, Max used the wall for support with one hand while clinging onto his hammer with the other.

Mad Max.

As he stood there swaying, everything quietened. A rare second of stillness before the smallest sound burst through it. A sniff. Someone ahead of him. At first it sounded like they might have a cold, but when they sniffed again, it seemed more intentional than that. An investigative sniff. They were testing the corridor to see what lurked there.

Max took a step towards the sound and they sniffed harder. "I don't know you," a woman said. "Who are you?"

"Huh?"

"What kind of a name is that?"

"I'm not one of the guards."

"That's not much of a name either. Do you understand questions? Also, even if you were a guard, you'd deny it. You're on your own; the last thing you want to do is mark yourself as the enemy. I suppose it doesn't matter who you are because I probably won't believe the truth even if I do hear it."

"It's true, I'm not a guard. Grandfather Jacks' palace has fallen. There are diseased everywhere outside. I have a friend in here."

"She might not be your friend anymore."

"Huh?"

"This place changes people."

A scream called to them from deep within the asylum. It came in rasping waves. Again and again until it slowly died, the will draining from the person with each call.

"See!" the woman said. "I can guarantee you she didn't sound like that when she came in here. None of them do."

"Who are you?" Max said.

"I'm not sure I know that anymore. And I'm not sure it matters anyway. I am who I am. You are who you are. Both of us are in the situation we're in, and both of us need to deal with what's in front of us right now."

Max reached out and gripped the bolt on her cell door in a pinch. Like with the one on the boy's cell, he wiggled it, the action gritty with rust.

"I wouldn't do that," the woman said.

"Huh?"

"You say that a lot, don't you?"

Max bit back his urge to say it again.

"You don't want to open this cell. You don't want to open any of them. You don't know what's behind these doors."

"Are you alone in there?"

"No, sweetie." Her voice was soft. Maternal. "And trust me, you don't want to open this Pandora's box."

"Then what shall I do?"

"I don't know. I don't know what your plan is, and I don't care to know, but I can tell you what you shouldn't do."

"What's that?"

"You shouldn't sit around feeling sorry for yourself. No one's going to show you a way out. You need to find it on your own. If the world outside is as you say it is, then no one's coming to rescue you, so sitting around is only going to give you a sore arse and a slow death."

"She's right, you know," Max said to himself.

"Huh?" the woman said.

"You sound like me!"

The woman tutted. "The madness in this place is as infectious as the disease. Get out of here while you still can."

"Thank you," Max said.

"You're welcome. And don't feel bad for me. For us."

"Why's that?"

"This cell isn't as bad as it looks. We get a lot of daylight in here."

The woman had clearly lost her mind. After looking left and right, Max said, "Huh?"

"Compared to most anyway. I saw you come in. I see everyone come in."

"What? Why didn't you tell me that? Where does the daylight come from?"

When the woman didn't say anything, Max said, "Are you pointing?"

"Sorry, sweetie." The woman laughed. "It comes from my right."

"Thank you." Max followed the woman's direction by turning to his left.

Steps as uncertain as any he'd taken in this place. Hard to trust the woman, but at least it gave him something to go on.

Tonk!

Max stepped back and rubbed his forehead. Not the first time he'd walked head first into a barrier, but at least he hadn't hit a stone wall. His hands out in front of him, he felt the cold steel door. The big handle, the small metal panel surrounding the keyhole. No window like the ones in the cells. The woman had been right. He'd nearly given up so close to his exit.

Walking his hands along the stone wall to his left, Max moved towards the cell where he'd left the key. When he found the wall, he turned a right angle and found the door. It swung open when he shoved it, letting him into what appeared to be one of the only abandoned cells in the place.

Max entered the cell, testing every step forwards with a lifted boot, waving it in the air until he caught the wooden bunk at the back.

The lip beneath it, the key he'd left there resting on the small ledge, Max nodded to himself and smiled. "Amazing!" He kissed the key and left the cell with the same tentative steps.

Back to the large exit door, Max found the small metal plate surrounding the keyhole again. A couple of taps before he found the hole and slotted the key home, twisted, and freed the lock with a loud *clack!*

The larger hinges on this door cackled like a smug crow as Max brought daylight into the asylum, his eyes watering, a lump in his throat.

The air was infinitely fresher outside, even with the diseased gathered around the tunnel, curdling it like soured milk. Max stepped into the sun's light and filled his lungs.

Barp! Max jumped on the spot, the loud foghorn tone calling across the wastelands. The diseased outside the steel tunnel yelled, snapped their heads in the direction of the sound, and set off.

The screams of the inmates in the asylum rose a notch, the tone streaking through the previously dark corridors. The lights had come on inside, small bulbs hanging from the walls about every ten feet or so.

Barp!

"Amazing!" Max said, turning to the palace. "Well done, guys." Although his heart sank as he said it. He'd have to go back in. If only he could talk to them and decide their best plan of action. But he already knew it. It would take a while for the diseased to clear before the others could cross the meadow to join him. They didn't have time. Matilda's thigh probably wasn't getting any better. They'd gone to the effort of getting the power on, so he had no choice but to go back in. The sooner he freed Dianna, the sooner they'd all be able to get the hell out of there and maybe help Matilda find something to heal her wound.

"Are you sure you want to go back in?" Max asked himself.

"It's not about what I want to do. It's about what I need to do. And at least it isn't dark in there anymore." A shake of his head, Max filled his lungs with the outside air. Best to make the most of it before he reentered the hellish building.

CHAPTER 11

William waited in the courtyard until just he and Cyrus remained. After tossing Jezebel up onto the tiles, he bent down and linked his hands to give Cyrus a boost. But the boy shook his head. "I can manage on my own, thank you."

William pulled a tight-lipped smile and stood aside.

A low window ledge in front of them, diseased on the other side of the thick glass. Their lips dragged along the transparent barrier while their teeth clicked against it as if they could bite their way through. Cyrus stepped onto the ledge like the others before him, jumped up, and caught the guardrail running along the edge of the roof.

A boost would have been a hell of a lot easier, the boy grunting as he swayed, struggling to lift his own weight. The desire to help sent twitches through William's muscles, but he fought the urge to get involved, stepping back even farther while the boy struggled.

When Cyrus had finally climbed clear, William followed him up in a fraction of the time, the guardrail damp from where his friend had sweated with the effort of his climb.

The roof's edge had several holes along it where tiles used to be. William stepped over them towards Matilda. He reached out and held her clammy hand. Although he raised his eyebrows, before he could ask her anything, the sound came again. A deep industrial tone, it called to the diseased in the area. *Barp!*

"I never thought I'd be glad to hear that noise again," Olga said. She squinted against the morning sun, her attention on the large ugly stone building across the meadow. "How do you think Max is getting on?"

"A lot better now he can see," Hawk said.

"Well done, gang," William said.

Olga put her hands on her hips. "That was reckless, William."

A dip of his head, he said, "I'm sorry."

"What good is sorry if one of us had been killed?" Hawk said.

"What good is a detailed plan when Matilda's running out of time?" William let go of his love's hand and pointed at her thigh. "Look at her leg."

Her face pale and sweating, Matilda shuffled on the spot with the discomfort of being the centre of attention. Fresh bloodstains seeped through the bandage on her thigh.

"So what do we do now?" Artan said. "Matilda needs our help, and I can't imagine Max is having much fun in that place."

"We can't possibly think about getting to the asylum at the moment," William said. "Firstly, how the hell will we get across to it? And secondly, Matilda needs to be our priority now. We've done what we can for Max for the time being."

Hawk drew his knife from his belt with such speed, it cut through the air with a *swish!* He aimed the tip at William, who tightened his grip on Jezebel's handle. "What the hell are you doing?"

"Stand aside, William. I have no beef with you."

Cyrus behind him, William turned to the meek boy before shrugging. "What the hell has Cyrus done?"

"Show them," Hawk said.

Because Cyrus always stood with a pathetic hunch, William hadn't noticed how he clenched his right hand. The boy's sweat on the guardrail hadn't been sweat. Were his skin not so dark, William would have seen it sooner. "That's why you didn't want help getting up? You were trying to hide that from us?"

A quivering bottom lip, his brown eyes glazed. Cyrus' shoulders rounded as he pulled into himself and shrugged. "I think it's just a cut. I got it when holding the gate closed, but I don't think they bit me."

Hawk flicked his knife in Cyrus' direction. "Why hide it, then?"

A half shout, half plea, Cyrus' voice broke when he said, "I got scared. I was worried you'd react like this."

Although William hadn't let go of Jezebel, he relaxed his grip and held his free hand at Hawk in a halting gesture. "What are you planning on doing?"

The whites of Hawk's eyes stood out. "We cut him down. We can't risk him turning."

"Wait a minute," Artan said. Then he stepped closer to Hawk, blocking his path to Cyrus. The hunter raised his knife. The point an inch from his throat, Artan said, "Calm down, will you?"

Hawk moved the tip even closer.

"This is why we had to rescue your arses," Olga said, rolling her eyes at Matilda. "Why don't you all rein in your egos and talk like civilised human beings?"

But Hawk remained fixed on Artan. "I will not calm down. I've lost people to the disease. I'm not prepared to take the risk."

Artan's tone remained even, and he maintained eye contact with Hawk as he spoke slow and deliberate words. "We've all lost people to the disease. That's what living in this world is. But we don't yet know if he's been bitten, and we've also seen someone get bitten and not turn. Had they killed Max when the diseased got him, I think I can safely say we would have all died a long time ago. Also, no one would be in the asylum looking for Dianna right now. So we wait, okay? We let Cyrus stand on his own, and we wait to see what happens to him. If he turns, there are enough of us to take him down."

Cyrus turned sideways to pass between William and Olga. He moved Artan aside and leaned his throat close to the tip of Hawk's blade. "You're right to be worried. I'll stand here, and if I turn, please kill me." Tears ran two glistening lines on his dark cheeks. "I don't want to be one of them. I'm sure none of us do."

"Can I also suggest," William said, "that when all this dick swinging's over"—he winked at Hawk—"maybe you can put on a shirt? If we're going to spend more time together, I'd prefer it if you weren't semi-naked."

Hawk's lip rose in a snarl before he turned back to Cyrus, fixing the boy with unblinking eyes. His knife shook and his knuckles turned white.

Despite his flippant comments about the shirt, William's pulse raced and his throat dried. He couldn't lose someone else. He gulped as he moved back to be with Matilda and whispered, "I hope Cyrus is okay."

"Me too," Matilda said. "Me too."

"William," Hawk said while he remained fixed on Cyrus, "once we've sorted this issue out, I want to take you somewhere."

William let go of Matilda's hand and stepped closer to the squat hunter. "What are you talking about?"

"I spent a lot of time in this place as a kid. I got a lot of wounds while I was here, as you can see." Despite the strong winds now they were higher up again, Hawk didn't seem affected by the cold.

"I didn't ask for your life story," William said.

"All of Grandfather Jacks' angels suffered a lot of wounds. A lot of wounds means a lot of infections."

"Where are you going with this?"

"They have an ointment in the palace."

William's jaw fell. "*What?*"

"They have—"

"I heard you." William's grip tightened on Jezebel's handle again and he worked his jaw, forming the shapes of the words before he finally found them. "Why the hell didn't you tell me sooner?"

"I'm telling you now."

William's voice broke. "So where do we find it?"

"Once we've dealt with Cyrus, I'll show you."

CHAPTER 12

Barp!

Max stood outside the asylum, the door still open, the poorly lit corridor stretching away from him. Even with the bulbs' glow, the darkness won out, the main hallway mostly shadow with weak splashes of light.

The outside air might have been curdled with the reek of the diseased, but Max would take a tainted cool breeze over the damp stagnation of the asylum.

Barp!

The sound came as if the vast building had gained sentience. It stood as the alpha on the landscape, its loud tone a challenge to anyone who felt up to it. Enter and see what happened.

A sea of diseased between Max and the palace, but he could still see the turrets and tiles that made up the grand building's roof. How were the others getting on? Had anything happened between Olga and Hawk? Had they kissed again?

A shake of his head, Max moved his war hammer from one hand to the other. Those thoughts didn't serve him.

Although, the same could be said of many of his current thoughts. "And they won't do that anyway." He had to say it aloud to get it past the voice in his head. The one that had control over the mental showreel with the two of them wrapped in each other's arms. "No!" he said. "They won't be doing that."

Mad Max.

The face of his oldest brother stared at Max from outside the steel tunnel. Greg. Over ten years older than him, he'd been more like a second dad than an older brother. By the time Mad Max was building his reputation as the nuttiest of the lot, he was getting ready to go on national service. When he came back, he went straight to work, so Max barely got to know him.

The face of the diseased Greg twisted as if it felt pity. Sad about how his little brother had turned out.

Mad Max.

But his mouth hadn't moved.

Mad Max.

"Why don't you piss off, Greg?"

The sudden change sent Max stumbling back several steps. The face of his brother altered. A dent in his skull, his eyeball swollen, his jaw hanging loose. Max turned away and covered his face with his hands. When he looked back again, the woman he'd been fixed on revealed herself. Shorter than Greg. Fatter. Female.

"What the fuck?" Max slammed his palm against his head again. He berated himself through gritted teeth. "I need to get a handle on this."

Maybe he should go back to the palace. Go check on everyone to see how they were doing. Make sure they were okay. Maybe chat to Olga. Show her he was worth waiting for. If she even wanted to wait for him. And who could blame her if she didn't? Hawk was a strapping lad and a fierce warrior. And he could give her a physical relationship.

Mad Max.

Speaking aloud so he could hear himself better, Max said, "But what would it look like for me to return without Dianna? How would that impress anyone? Especially when they'd gone to the effort of getting the power back on."

The poorly lit corridors stretched away from him on his left. The palace across the sea of diseased in front of him. Space, open air, his friends. But Dianna was only fourteen. She didn't deserve to be in there. And what about the children?

Barp!

The monotonous sound surged through the corridors. What must it be like to be trapped in there?

As the echoes of the deep bark faded, the screams of the inmates rose in volume. They didn't deserve to be incarcerated. He could help them. His mum always said that if he could help someone in need, then he should.

Barp!

In the aftermath of the next tone, the screams died down to be replaced with a chorus of sobbing children. Alone and broken. Now Grandfather Jacks had gone, their lives should be infinitely better. But how were they to know that? When had they last eaten? Who provided for them in his absence?

One last look at the palace. He trusted Olga. Not that she needed his trust or asked for it. She could do what the hell she liked and she damn well would. But she cared about him. She'd shown him she wanted to make it work.

His heart pulling towards the palace, his head pulling back into the asylum, Max shook his war hammer. "Dammit!"

Max re-entered the asylum on leaden legs. He pulled the door closed behind him, slid the key back in the lock, the *clack* of the securing door running away from him into the darkness.

Barp!

Now inside, the sound rattled through Max's skeleton. What must it have been like to spend any time incarcerated in this place? No wonder they were all so batshit crazy. Had they already lost Dianna to her own spiralling thoughts? Too much time in here would send anyone into mental decline.

He returned to the cell he'd hid the key in before. It contained just a wooden bed. It reeked of mould. As Max bent down by the bed and felt for the ledge beneath the wooden bench, he turned back to the door. Surely just paranoia about being watched. But what if some of the inmates were already loose? What if they'd stayed put because they couldn't see where they were going, but now the lights were on … He had his hammer. That would have to do.

His hands shaking, Max dropped the key, the small piece of metal hitting the stone floor with a tinkle. A delicate noise in a place where everything else was turned up to eleven. One eye still on the door, he patted the cold stone floor, missing the key several times before he slapped his hand over it again.

Barp!

Adrenaline surging through him, Max drew steadying breaths. He put all his attention on hiding the key before darting for the cell's exit.

The hall might have been bathed in shadow, but some light was better than none. If there were any loose inmates, at least he'd stand a chance of defending himself.

Barp!

The war hammer held slightly away from his body, ready to swing should anyone jump him. How far would he have to walk through this place before he found Dianna? A particularly shrill scream ran a shiver down his spine. More children sobbed. Did he really have this in him?

But did he really have a choice? If you can help someone in need, then you should. He'd never see his mum again, but if she looked down on him at that moment, she'd want him to follow his current course. To free the innocent. He'd been allowed to live for a reason. He'd been the one in a million who was immune for a reason. He owed it to what remained of this wretched world to share his gift.

And how bad would it be?

Barp!

More screams.

Having not moved since he'd stepped from the cell with the key, Max nodded to himself. "If you can help someone in need." Then a second time. "If you can help someone in need." He stepped forward, deeper into the asylum, fighting every urge in his body to leave. He could help, so he should.

CHAPTER 13

"Come on, man," William said, throwing his arms away from his body, Jezebel in his right grip. "We've been here for about fifteen minutes with you holding that damn knife to Cyrus' throat. When have you ever known it to take *this* long for someone to turn?"

Barp! The tone from the asylum continued to call the diseased to prayer. The breeze carried their rancid reek.

As he'd done for the entire time, Hawk kept his harsh frown fixed on Cyrus. "It does no harm to make sure."

William's pulse quickened and he drew a deep breath in through his nose. "Unless you're Matilda."

Olga stepped forwards and rested a hand on Hawk's bare back. The muscles along his side twitched. "William's right," she said. "It's been long enough. He would have turned by now."

The blade at the end of Hawk's outstretched arm remained an inch from Cyrus' throat. It wobbled, maybe from the strain of holding it, maybe from the tension in his white-knuckled grip. He finally yielded, lowering the knife, letting his tightly wound shoulders relax.

"Right," William said, "so now you've finally finished, and now we've all risked our lives to save your friend's life—"

"Dianna's a good person. I wouldn't be here if it weren't for her."

"That's all well and good," William said, "but my point still stands. We've helped you achieve what you wanted, so how about you do us a favour now and take us to the ointment?"

"You understand that we had to put the electricity back online first, right?" Hawk said. "It was a quick and easy problem to solve. And fixing it will have a great impact. Had I told you about the ointment, there's no way you would have come here with us, and we needed you."

"You clearly did. Without me, you would have taken hours trying to work out the best route to the batteries, and Matilda would have died a slow and painful death." Spittle sprayed from William's mouth when he said, "Although, I'm still not convinced she's going to avoid that. Can we just get on with finding the ointment?"

Hawk raised a halting finger at William. "Now—"

"I swear, the only reason I haven't buried this axe in your head is because we need you."

The steel he'd grown used to seeing in Hawk's glare returned and his upper body tensed. The scars around his neck shifted with his twitching pecs. But then he relaxed and dropped his attention to his feet. "You're right. I'm sorry. I have been delaying. It's not that I don't care about Matilda, and it's not that I don't appreciate the help to get the power back on. It's just …" He looked up, his usual certainty absent, a glaze of tears staring back at William. "It's where we have to go to get the ointment."

William's throat burned, the withheld scream itching for release. "I don't care where it is if it's going to make Matilda feel better. It could be in the deepest darkest corner of hell."

"I'd rather it was there, if I'm being honest."

Since William had met Hawk, he'd been certain about everything. He'd had the certainty of a fool. He'd been pigheaded and unflinching in what he had to do. But that certainty came from fear. The world closed in around him on a daily basis, and if he didn't convince himself he was in control, he'd crumble. For the first time, Hawk openly wore that fear. After resting Jezebel on the tiles head first, the handle standing up between them, William reached over and grabbed the top of Hawk's arms. "Whatever it is, we'll get there, and we'll support you. But please, we can't hang around any longer. I can't lose Matilda. I'm sure you understand that?"

Hawk dipped his head in concession and said, "Okay."

"Cyrus," William said, "we're going to leave you here with Matilda."

"I can look after mys—" Matilda paused and took several deep breaths, her face locked in a frown against her clear pain.

William looked at Cyrus. "You stay here, okay?"

Cyrus nodded.

A guardrail close by, William tugged at it, ripping it free from the edge of the roof. He handed the cold metal bar to Cyrus.

"What am I supposed to do with this?"

"Use it if you need it. Hawk needs your sword."

"I'm not taking a sword," Hawk said. He brandished his spear. He also had a knife similar to Artan's.

Olga raised an eyebrow. "You're planning on throwing spears inside the palace?"

The muscles along the side of Hawk's face twitched as he clenched his jaw. Artan handed his spears to Matilda. In the tight corridors of the building below, they'd only be a hinderance.

Hawk gave Artan his knife so the boy had one for each

hand. He then took Cyrus' sword. "Thank you. I'll make sure I return it."

"Just be sure to come back," Cyrus said.

As Hawk led the others away, William crouched down in front of Matilda, held her face with both of his hands, and kissed her. He breathed in, inhaling every last moment of their connection. "We'll be back in time with the ointment, I promise."

A weak smile, Matilda said, "I love you."

William kissed her again. "I love you too." He took off after the others along the slightly slanted roof.

The asylum continued to call the diseased. *Barp!* Hopefully those in the palace heard it loud and clear. Maybe a naive wish, but they could do with the building being empty of those damn creatures.

CHAPTER 14

There were many people in need in the asylum, but Max had to get Dianna out of there first. His number one priority before she became one of the shrieking chorus wailing in the shadows. A two-handed grip on his war hammer, his body tense from where the cold walls pressed in on him, he kept walking forwards. One foot in front of the other. One step at a time.

Barp!

Already cold and shivering in the asylum, Max's body made it worse by releasing a shot of adrenaline every time the tone sounded. The noise counted down without end. At least without an end he knew of. This building probably knew exactly when Max would crumble. Put him in a field of diseased and, although he might see his siblings as he cracked skulls, he could cope. But nothing up until this point had prepared him for this place. Children and women sobbing in the darkness. Never-ending stone corridors, heady with cloying damp infused with waste and sweat. How long would he have to wander the hallways searching for Dianna? Was she even here?

Barp!

"So you got the lights back on?" said the woman in the cell who'd shown Max the exit.

Max stepped closer, the weak bulbs in the hallway revealing more of her face. Her black matted hair clung to her greasy skin. Many of her teeth were missing. There were more gaps than enamel when she opened her mouth. His natural instinct to pull away from this grotesque woman, his body still shaking with the surges of adrenaline, he said, "Uh … thank you for helping me get out."

While the woman's external appearance personified madness, her eyes shone with a deep warmth and humanity. This place hadn't gotten to her yet. A grin filled with gaps, she nodded. "You're welcome."

Barp!

Max flinched when the woman moved to the left, the weak light catching the sore on her right cheek. Black with age, it had eaten a hole in the side of her face. How much longer before it started on the bones beneath? Maybe if he got her out, she could clean herself? A thick rusting bolt stood between this woman and liberation.

The woman must have followed his line of sight because she moved aside, allowing the light in the cell behind her to highlight the six or seven silhouettes waiting in the shadows. Maybe one or two of them were children, but the majority were adults.

Max backed away. There were too many unknowns back there. Let them out and he might never reach Dianna. If he could help, he should, but should he help to the detriment of what he hoped to achieve?

The woman winked and spoke in a low hiss so only Max heard her. "Good choice."

The woman vanished from where she got shoved aside, another inmate crashing into the door with a *slam!*

Wild eyes stared from the small window. A fat face framed by matted and greasy hair. Thick bags beneath her dark eyes, she spoke with a deep voice. "Let us out of here now!"

Max took another step away.

The woman who'd spoken to him first said, "Don't let them out."

The new woman kicked the door.

Barp!

She grabbed the bars in the small window and shook them, the door rattling in its frame. "Let us out of here! Who the hell are *you* to play god?"

Max moved back another pace. The larger woman also stepped back. Although he couldn't see into the cell, the thud and gasp of someone being winded came out to him. Max stepped closer. "What are you doing to her?"

"Let us out," the new woman said, "otherwise she dies."

While wringing the wooden handle of his war hammer, Max ground his jaw. He'd stand a good chance against the larger woman with his weapon. But how could he start fighting the inmates? They were the victims in this. And would they really hurt one of their own? "I will be back to let everyone out," Max said.

"How can we trust you?" the mean woman said.

"You have no choice."

"We can choose to beat this woman to a pulp."

"And I can choose to leave you in this cell to rot."

Max's legs trembled as he stumbled away. Hopefully he wouldn't have to follow through on his threat.

∽

Barp!

The tone ran to Max's core. Instead of getting used to it,

the noise peeled back another layer of skin and jabbed him harder than before. How long had some of the women been in here? Did they all lose their minds after a certain time? No wonder the corridors were filled with sobs and screams.

Mad Max.

"No!" Max hit his head with the heel of his right palm. "Not now. Not in here."

"Hey, guard!"

Not the first one to shout that at him, Max refused to look at where the call came from. Instead, he stared ahead down the long corridor. "I'm not a guard."

"Come on, guard, let us out of here. At least give us some food. I'll do whatever you want. Please."

Cells lined the shadowy corridor, and more women called at him. "Come on, we haven't been fed in days."

And it probably felt like days to them, but the place had only fallen the previous day. Whatever happened, they probably had a little bit longer before they worried about starvation.

"Guard, guard, please let us out." A woman on his left.

"Come on." A woman on his right.

Barp!

"Open up. Don't leave us to die in here."

"We're loyal to Grandfather Jacks."

"Grandfather Jacks is dead!" Max threw his arms wide, the weight of his hammer in his right hand. While gripping the handle, he shook the weapon in the direction of the last woman to call to him. "He's been killed, and I have *nothing* to do with him."

"Then let us out, guard!"

Were it anyone but a child, Max would have walked away. The small face pressed to the bars of a cell on his left. Dirty cheeks, deep brown eyes flickering with torment. Sanity resided in that small skull, but for how much longer?

"Please. I need to get out of here." The kid's mahogany stare glazed, filling with tears.

Barp!

Every part of Max's being pulled towards the small child. He didn't deserve this. He needed to let him out. But where did he draw the line if he did? How many more children would ask to be freed? How many adults would he have to liberate?

"No." Max shook his head and backed away. "I can't let you out. Not right now. I'm sorry."

"Guard!" The shouts started up again.

"Please, guard, we don't deserve this."

"Let us out."

Barp!

Mad Max.

Max's breaths grew shallow, his chest tight. More and more cries for help, they swirled through the air around him. How the hell was he supposed to find Dianna in this chaos?

"Guard!"

And if they thought he was a guard, what would they do to him if he let them all out?

"Dianna!" Max shouted. It silenced those around him.

Barp!

He tried again. "Dianna? Dianna? Where are you?"

"I'm Dianna!" A small child's voice. A boy.

"I'm Dianna!" A woman on his right.

More and more of them said they were Dianna. Other than the screams and shouts, other than the tears of the tormented children, every voice laid claim to that moniker. He'd not thought it through. And how could he tell if one of them was Dianna? So dark he'd have to get closer to every cell. Get the women to show their faces. Engage with their insanity.

Barp!

"Max!"

Max stopped. "Dianna?"

"Max! What are you doing here? I thought—"

"We were dead?"

"I'm so sorry." Dianna's voice broke. "If any of us had told you what they had planned for you in Umbriel, they would have killed us and everyone we loved."

Maybe she'd made the correct decision, and maybe she hadn't. All that mattered right now was getting her out of her cell and back to the others. For both of them to get away from this hellish place.

Barp!

Max switched his war hammer to his left hand and reached up, tugging on the bolt with his right. Best to clear the air before he let Dianna out. She'd only acted in the way she thought most appropriate. And what would he have done at fourteen if he'd lived the same life as her? "We got away. Me, Cyrus, William, and Artan."

"That's great news. I'm sorry they even did that to you."

"We have Hawk with us. He's been helping us, and he's set on getting you out of here. That's why I've come back. Turns out he's not as loyal to Grandfather Jacks as many others were."

The bolt's action was gritty as he worked it free. *Clack!* Like every set of hinges in this place, the ones for Dianna's cell door were no different, groaning as if even they were tormented from spending too much time in the asylum.

Dianna stood in the doorway. But then she vanished into the darkness. Her arms flailed as someone behind dragged her back. Another pair of hands shot from the cell, grabbed Max by his shirt, and pulled him in. Light exploded through his vision, the headbutt driving fire through his sinuses. Dizzy from the blow, his legs failed him as the shadows closed in.

CHAPTER 15

*B*arp!

William watched his step, the part of the roof they now crossed leaning at enough of an angle for it to be problematic should he stand on a loose tile. Yet he kept looking out into the meadow, the diseased flocking to the sound from the asylum. Like ants storming a picnic, they moved as one to the saccharine lure of the monotone call. "Should make it easier to go through the palace."

Artan walked beside William, his back straight, his chin raised. "Let's hope so."

Hawk and Olga several steps ahead of them, Hawk said, "We need to clear the air."

William nearly spoke until he realised Hawk meant for only Olga to hear him. The short girl looked the hunter up and down. "We do?"

"W-what happened in Umbriel. It came out of nowhere. And while it was fun, I don't want it to get in the way of you and Max."

"There is no me and Max." Olga then quickly added, "But

it's fine. Honestly. I'm not into you either. I mean, don't get me wrong, you're—"

Hawk's smile cut her off. He squinted in the strong wind. He reached out to Olga, and for a moment the pair squeezed hands before letting them drop. "Thank you."

"And what about you and Dianna?" Olga said.

At first it had made William uncomfortable to listen to their conversation; he now sped up to be sure he didn't miss any of it.

Hawk shook his head. "She's young. She's only fourteen. She's more like a little sister, you know?"

"How come you're so close?" Olga said.

"We just get on well." After a second of staring into space, Hawk added, "She supported me when I needed it most." His hand went to the rope burns around his neck. "Had she not found me when she did …" His glazed eyes lost focus. "And it wasn't just about her finding me at the right time, it was the support she gave me after. She came to me every day to see how I was doing." He smiled, his eyes remaining unfocused while his voice wavered. "She had a knack of always being there when things got bad."

Desperate for something to say, William's mind went blank. But it didn't stop the crucial questions. He'd already doubted Hawk's intentions, but even if his intentions were good, could they trust him? Was his head in the right place to be leading them into the palace?

Hawk walked to the edge of the roof and lay on his front, leaning over the side. William and the others did the same, the guardrail pressing into his chest from where he lay across it.

"That's one of Grandfather Jacks' private rooms," Hawk said.

Several diseased on the ground snarled up at them. Two

men, three women, and a young boy. They reached out as if they could will the group to fall.

"Grandfather Jacks always left the window ajar." Hawk continued. "Whenever he took me into this room, I'd stare at the small gap. An inch of daylight, nothing more, but it would be enough to inspire dreams of freedom. Who'd have thought—" he laughed a humourless laugh "—after all that time wishing I could climb out of the window, that I'd be using this gap to get back *into* the palace?"

While Hawk spoke in monotone, his face twisted and his brow pinched. Could they really trust him to take them into this place? What if he'd already lost his mind? "Why should we go in this way?" William said.

"It's a small and private room. Unlike many of the rooms in the building, you have to press the button beside the door three times to open it. With all these automatic doors, the diseased will be going wherever they like. Grandfather Jacks built these rooms for privacy, and I'd wager that not even the smartest diseased will work out how to enter."

Were William not leaning so close to Hawk, he might not have noticed him trembling. "Are you sure you're okay to do this?"

Hawk got up onto his knees and gripped the guardrail. His mouth spread into a maniacal grin. Panic sat in his glare. He jumped, swung around with the guardrail, and slammed both feet into the window frame, breaking it open with a splintering crash. In one fluid movement, he vanished into the room, the diseased on the ground throwing their arms up with an angry flurry.

A strangled diseased wail from inside the place, Olga said, "Oh shit!" She swung around and followed Hawk in.

Jezebel in one hand, William hung down from the guardrail with the other, found the window ledge with his right foot and then his left before he climbed into the room after his friends.

One diseased ran from one side of the room to the other, evading Hawk's attack. As it ran past the window, William kicked it in the side of the head with a *clop!*

The diseased fell to the ground and Olga finished it off by driving the point of her sword into its right ear. It squelched when she pulled it back out again. Four diseased lay on the floor, a pool of crimson spreading out beneath them.

William jumped into the room, his feet hitting the tiled floor with a *crack*. He stood aside so Artan could slide in after him. The small space was no more than about eight feet square. Empty save for a bed along one wall and a wardrobe. There were straps at each corner of the bed.

While Olga fought to catch her breath, Hawk stood dead still, his attention on the bed, tears filling his eyes. Wherever he was at that moment, he wasn't in the room with the rest of them.

The cupboard door creaked when William opened it. The sight sent him stumbling back. Whips and chains hung down from the coat rail inside.

Still nothing from Hawk. He continued staring at the bed, his hands shaking as he rubbed the scars on his neck and chest.

Olga put a hand on Hawk's back and the boy jumped, dragging a sharp intake of breath. "Come on," she said, "let's get the hell out of here."

As if trying to get himself started, Hawk nodded several times. It took a few more seconds for him to turn his back on the source of his torment. He hovered near the button to exit the room and said, "I'm going to open this door. I'm hoping the tone from the asylum has pulled a lot of the diseased away. Directly opposite this room is a door leading to the basement."

"This place has a basement?" Artan said.

A sardonic smile, Hawk said, "It's not somewhere they advertise in the brochure. It's where the ointment is. I'm hoping the diseased are yet to discover it."

"You ready for this?" Olga said.

Hawk nodded, but he stepped aside. He clearly needed someone else to lead.

"One …" Olga said, her hand over the button.

"Two …

"Three …" She slapped the button three times, the door opening, screams from the diseased flooding into the room.

Hawk charged out first, leading with his sword. He drove the closest diseased back by burying the tip into its face. After kicking it free from his blade, he went to work, slashing, stabbing, and cutting. He used Ranger's old sword like he'd been born to wield it.

Blood splashed on the white tiled floor. Olga followed Hawk out, keeping her distance from him and taking down the diseased on the periphery of his chaotic attack.

Artan went out next, William grabbing several long chains from the cupboard before he too entered the larger hallway.

If William joined the battle, he'd just get in the way. Six to eight diseased remained, and while his friends cut them down, he used one of the long chains and tied the door to the private room shut. A handle on the door and one on the wall next to it, even with the three button presses, it made sense to secure their escape route.

"What the hell are you doing?" Hawk said, blood dripping from the tip of his sword. While he watched William, Artan and Matilda continued fighting the creatures around them.

"I want to make sure no more diseased get in here while we're away." The air reeked with the rotten stench of diseased. "We need to keep a clear path for a quick retreat."

Artan, who danced through the diseased with a blade in each hand, wedged the tips of both knives into the eyes of a diseased. When he pulled the blades from its face, he drew out two lines of blood and the creature fell. He slapped Hawk on the back with a loud *crack* and said, "Come on, we need to keep moving."

The hunter turned his back on William. Artan raised his eyebrows at his friend.

Maybe the chains had been a bad choice, but they were effective. William shrugged, finished tying the doors, and crossed the blood-soaked hallway to be with the others. Double wooden doors covered the basement's entrance. No automation here.

Were it not for the *barp* in the distance, they would have been overwhelmed in the wide corridor. Maybe Hawk had been correct about the electricity being a priority. Maybe they could rely on him.

The cries of more diseased rang through the corridors. Instead of quickening his pace so they could get out of there, Hawk turned and faced the direction of the sound. He raised his sword in preparation for the fight, even though they had the chance to escape. William sighed. Then again, maybe they couldn't.

CHAPTER 16

B*arp!*
The first thing Max heard when he came to. The bone-rattling tone surged through the dark corridors of the labyrinthine asylum.

A throbbing headache ran through both of Max's eyeballs, a bulb close to his face, bright because of its proximity. It glowed in his eye, blinding him to the rest of the room. It gave off a small amount of heat against his cheek. It made it hard to judge the size of the cell. His hands were above his head, strapped to a wooden baton, the ropes at his wrists and ankles tied so tightly they burned.

Max's right hand closed around thin air as he grabbed for where his war hammer had once been. When he shook his arms, the wooden baton and metal chains above him rattled.

A dry funk in his mouth, fur on his tongue, Max gulped against the stale and metallic taste of his own blood. A large patch of it had turned the front of his shirt crusty.

Barp!

Women screamed and children cried.

Unable to stifle his cough, Max released a deep barking

hack, the sting in his eyeballs so intense they felt like they might burst.

Nothing but Max and the shadows. Until she stepped forwards. Had she been there the whole time?

"So he's awake!" The woman stepped so close the weak bulb beside Max lit up her face too. She had pale skin, greasy brown hair, and oversized yellow teeth. Five feet tall at the most, she looked like an oversized rat more than she did an undersized human. Eyes so dark the irises could have been black. She sniffed, her pointed nose just an inch from Max's right cheek. "I hate the guards who run this place."

"I'm not a guard!"

The woman's speed and the darkness of the cell meant the first Max knew of her kick was the stinging blow. Her toe connected clean, electricity streaking up the front of his leg before balling beneath his patella. Although he tried to twist to ease the sting, his bonds restricted his movement.

The woman kicked him again in exactly the same spot, and Max clamped his jaw, biting down on his scream.

Barp!

The woman remained close, panting hot and heavy halitosis on Max's face before she vanished back into the shadows. Were it not for her slathering respiration, he might have assumed she'd left. Max finally said, "Why are you attacking me? I told you I'm not a guard."

The woman burst from the shadows again. She cupped his crotch and moved so close to him their noses touched. Insanity swirled in the inky blackness of her wild glare. Her top lip rose in a snarl. It revealed more of her oversized teeth. She squeezed hard, her thin lips pulling back. She sprayed his face with spittle. "Don't lie to me. I've been in here too long. I've seen too many tricks to fall for any of your bullshit."

Cramps streaked from the woman's grip straight into

Max's bowels. He tried to ride out the pain with deep breaths. If arguing would have gotten him anywhere, he would have put up more of a fight. Clamping his eyes shut, tears leaked from them and ran down his cheeks. "H-h-how—"

The woman squeezed harder. "Spit it out!"

"How long have you been in here?"

Barp!

Although she kept her hand cupping his testicles and penis, she let go of the tight squeeze, and Max groaned with relief. The sharpness left her tone. "They brought me here when I was fourteen."

"Fourteen! That must have been—"

"Steady." She squeezed again, although not as hard this time. The whites of her eyes stood out on her face. "You should never ask a lady how old she is."

No doubt her time in the asylum had aged her by ten years, but even with that, she'd still clearly been in this place for longer than she'd spent outside it. "When was the last time you saw daylight?"

"I just told you, didn't I?"

Max pulled back as the woman surged forwards. Again, she spared him the gut-wrenching twist, letting go of his crotch completely. "They said I wasn't ever ready to receive Grandfather Jacks' wisdom. Do you know what I think?"

Max shook his head.

"I think they forgot about me for too long, and when they finally remembered, I wasn't young enough for the dirty old bastard. But I'll show him. I'll get out of here, and if I need to cut your throat as a message to him, I will."

"But Grandfather Jacks is dead," Max said.

"Don't lie to me."

Barp!

"I swear it, he is. The palace has fallen. Did you hear the sound go off? Did you see the lights go out?"

Her features softened.

"That was when he got killed and his palace fell. All of his guards have gone too."

While shaking her head, the woman stepped away. She clapped her hands to her face with a *crack* and held on as if it would help her contain her madness. "You're lying so I'll let you go. Then when I do, you'll overpower me."

This woman clearly couldn't be reasoned with.

Another woman stepped from the shadows. In her late teens to early twenties, she was slim, had a healthy glow to her cheeks, and held two cups of water. She handed one to the lady and said, "Here you go, Monica, drink this."

The woman raised the cup to her lips and drained it, her dark eyes levelled on Max the entire time. They dared him to aggravate her again.

His balls throbbing, a deep sting on his right shin, he clamped his jaw and waited. Let the woman speak. She probably had a lot to get off her chest, and she wouldn't believe what he had to say right now.

"What do you think, Gracie?" Monica kept her attention on Max.

"Huh?" the girl who'd brought in the water said.

"About this one. He claims he has nothing to do with Grandfather Jacks. That the palace and all the guards have fallen."

"Then why did he have keys on him? And why are we still locked in?"

Monica tilted her head to one side as if to relay the questions to Max. "She has a point."

"I took the keys from a guard."

"So where's the key to get out of here? We've tried every one on the key ring we took from you, and none of them work. The guards don't stay in here. They let several in at a time and lock them in. I think that's what's happened to you. Because if you came in on your own, surely you'd have the key to get out again?"

"I—"

"I think you're lying," Gracie said, cutting Max off. "I think we need to hold on to you and wait for someone to come to your rescue. I think you're a guard. And when they come for you, I think that'll be our ticket out of here."

Max's cheeks puffed out when he exhaled. He'd nearly told them about the key in the cell. Did this woman realise what she'd just done by revealing their plan? Now he couldn't tell them about the key to get out of there. As long as they thought someone would come and bust him out, they'd keep him alive.

It started low, bubbling from Monica's throat like water in a thirsty drain. It grew in volume and pace as her cackle ran away from her. Louder and faster, it gathered momentum before morphing into a scream. A wild monkey call, it rang so loud the rest of the asylum fell silent.

Barp!

She bounced on the spot, her wild eyes giddy before she charged Max and kicked him between the legs with a yell.

Max coughed several times in an attempt to manage the pain before he vomited down his front.

Her breathing ragged, her hair hanging across her sweating face, Monica snarled and paced back and forth in front of Max. "We'll keep you alive because we need you. But by the time we're done, you'll wish you were dead."

CHAPTER 17

The approaching diseased's footsteps beat an out-of-time rhythm as they closed down on their position. William and the others continued towards the doors leading to the basement, but Hawk stood waiting for them, his sword raised. He snapped his head from side to side as if trying to touch each ear against each shoulder, limbering up for the fight.

Although William opened his mouth to speak, what could he say to convince the hunter to join them? From the blank looks on Artan's and Olga's faces, they had nothing either.

Barp! The sound much quieter in the palace, but it still came through to them. "Uh, Hawk."

The diseased drew closer, Hawk turning his feet as if trying to improve the stability of his stance.

"Hawk," William tried again, "what are you doing, man? This isn't a fight we need to be having."

Hawk turned so quickly, William jumped back, lifting Jezebel a little higher should he need to fight. Deep wrinkles ran along Hawk's brow, his jaw tight.

His mouth dry, William adjusted his sweaty grip.

But Hawk's scowl lifted and he lowered his sword. He ran for the doors leading to the basement. A set of double doors without automation, Hawk kicked them hard enough to break the lock with the tearing rip of splintering wood.

As the last one in, William closed the doors and tied the handles with one of the chains he'd taken from Grandfather Jacks' comfort room. When he'd finished, he tugged on them, the chains rattling as the doors opened by no more than an inch.

A set of stairs led down to a shadowy hallway, most of the dark tunnel hidden from their sight from where it turned a ninety-degree left at the bottom. Small bulbs ran down either wall, a gap of about six feet between each. "At least we have the lights on now. Imagine doing this in the dark."

"I wouldn't," Hawk said, taking several steps down towards the gloomy corridor. "Which is why I insisted on getting the power on first."

"What about the other people?" Artan said.

Olga seemed keen to talk. Anything to break through the tension between them all. "What other people?"

"The ones who chased Max out of the palace."

"They're dead," Hawk said. "Didn't you see what happened?"

A moment's pause, Artan then replied with an even tone, "Of course I saw what happened, but what if there are more? It won't be hard for them to untie the chains."

"Worst case," William said, "our route back won't be safe. Best case, it will. We need to at least try to give ourselves the easiest route back to Matilda."

Artan's concerns had drawn Hawk's focus back to the chains. The stocky hunter glared at them, his breaths rocking through him in waves. "I don't appreciate them."

It took for the quiet between them all to hear the tone.

Barp!

"At least down here we don't have to listen to that," Olga said.

Hawk's expression deadpan, he looked back down the stairs. "If there were a choice, I'd take that annoying noise over where we're going all day long."

"So this is the right way?" Olga said.

When Hawk didn't answer, she took several tentative steps down the stairs and rested a hand on his shoulder. She pointed down. "This is the right way?"

Hawk remained statue still, pausing long enough for William to move from one foot to the other as if he could somehow wriggle free of his discomfort. Hawk finally nodded. "Uh ... yeah, this way. This way. Yeah."

Hawk led them down the stone stairs. A wide back glistening with sweat and as lashed with scars as the front. The snakelike scar wrapped around his neck from where the rope must have eaten into his flesh when Dianna found him.

The deeper they went, the thicker the damp in the air. The stone stairs leading to the basement were worn in the middle from what must have been years of use.

Artan grabbed William, halting his descent and forcing a gasp from him. After Hawk had gone down a few more steps, he spoke in a whisper. "Are you sure this is a good idea? Trusting Hawk to lead us, I mean?"

"Do we have any other choice?"

Although Artan looked like he had more to say, he simply shrugged, allowing William to continue after Hawk and Olga.

The wild scream of a diseased snapped William rigid. Olga froze in front of him, and Artan stepped back a pace. William raised Jezebel, Olga and Artan also holding their weapons ready to attack.

But instead of waiting for the diseased to come to them, Hawk hopped down several more steps.

"Looks like they're down here too," Olga said.

The uneven beat of footsteps came from the shadows around the bend. It ran down a tight tunnel towards them.

Hawk moved down several more steps, now just a few feet from the bottom.

"Hawk," William said, "what are you doing? Step back. We have a much better chance making that thing come to us."

The beast sounded barefoot. The slap of its steps patted the stone ground. If Hawk heard William, he hid it well.

"Hawk!" Olga tried this time. When he continued his descent, she turned back to the others and shrugged.

"What can we do?" William said.

"Follow him?" Artan said.

"No way." William shook his head. "What he's doing is suicide. Hawk, come back up here."

All the while, Hawk remained fixed on the gloomy tunnel. He opened his right hand, his sword hitting the stone stairs with a *ching!*

"What are you doing?" Olga said. "You can't fight that thing with your bare hands."

The creature so close William ruffled his nose at the vinegar tang. When Olga stepped closer to Hawk, he darted forwards and gripped the top of her arm, dragging her up the stairs. "Get back. We stay together in this. We'll only get the ointment and get back to the others if we work as a tea—"

The diseased burst around the corner with a shriek. A woman about five feet six inches tall. Hawk caught her around the throat, her dirty and matted brown hair falling across her face as he lifted her from the ground by her neck. Her feet swung in front of her when he drove her towards the ground, slamming her against the hard steps. It forced an "oomph" from her, and she fell limp for the briefest of moments.

The diseased woman twisted and shrieked. She kicked

out and waved her arms, desperate to be free of Hawk, who kept her pinned to the stone stairs.

The weak light shone off the side of Hawk's tense face. The muscles along his arms stood out like ropes. Sweat glistened on his body, and as much as the diseased fought to be free, she had no chance against his power. He could end her right now should he desire.

Instead, Hawk took his time. Saliva dripping from his gritted teeth, his face locked in a grimace that resembled a smile in all but spirit. The creature lost her fight. Acceptance? A lack of breath? Fatigue? Hard to tell.

But when Hawk let go, the creature did something William had never seen before. She ignored the uninfected human closest to her, scrambling away from him as she crawled up the stairs towards the others. Arachnid in her approach, her teeth snapped as she used both her arms and legs to drag herself towards Artan, Olga, and William.

Hawk caught her heels this time, grabbing them and pulling her back down the stairs. Her chin played the hard steps like a xylophone. He turned the creature over so she lay on her back. He sat on her chest, pinning her biceps beneath his knees, and pressed his thumbs into her eye sockets.

The thick muscles in Hawk's tight jaw bulged with his exertion. Two wet pops and the creature's eyes yielded to the pressure. The rancid reek of rot escaped her skull as she fell limp and slid down to the bottom of the stairs.

Without looking at them, Hawk wiped his hands on his trousers, picked up his sword, walked to the bottom of the stairs, stepped over the creature, and vanished around the corner into the dark tunnel.

Pale and slack jawed, Olga snorted a laugh. "I guess he doesn't like it down here, then?"

After a glance at Artan, William said, "This is our last chance. Shall we follow him?"

Artan nodded. "Whatever else he has going on, I think he'll take us to the ointment."

A shrug of her shoulders, Olga led the way.

Were they about to make an awful decision? But what other choice did they have? They didn't know this palace, and whether they liked it or not, Hawk was the most qualified to get them to their destination.

CHAPTER 18

Shortly after Monica's final attack on Max, she left. The bulb so close to Max's face it blinded him to anything in the shadows, so he had to trust what little he could see and hear. The *crack* of the door being locked behind her and then silence. Had he been left alone?

Max tasted his own blood in his throat, and the ache in his testicles still ran to the pit of his stomach. Connecting with the pain made him want to vomit.

Barp!

The sound continued, unrelenting in its deep and tormenting call.

Crack! The bolt on the other side of the door released. The hinges groaned, screams and shouts from the asylum entering with someone's footsteps. The chains above Max rattled when he pulled against his restraints. A futile attempt to break free, but the only power he currently had.

Like with his bonds, blinking did nothing to improve his situation. He remained blinded by the bulb's glare.

Gracie stepped into the light, and Max's tension left him.

She might still be an arsehole, but he would have chosen her over Monica all day long.

She stepped closer than when she'd been in the room with Monica, allowing Max to see her better. She had long ginger hair, which she wore in a thick plait that ran all the way down her back. She had kind eyes and soft features. "What do you want?" Max said.

"You should be grateful I'm not Monica."

"I am. That doesn't mean I trust you. I'd rather not be in this situation at all." Pins and needles ran down Max's arms from where they were suspended above his head, the ropes cutting into his wrists. "Also, if you lot are so against the guards, why do the one thing to me that you hate? Why restrain me and lock me up, and why are you leaving those women and children locked in their cells too?"

"We're feeding them."

Barp!

"Just like the guards would? Why become the very people you hate?"

"Monica has."

"You're different, are you?"

Gracie revealed the cup of water she'd brought with her. Her brilliant white-toothed smile disarmed him. "Are you thirsty?"

Max shrugged and swallowed a dry gulp. He lost his words and coughed to bring them back. "Don't go out of your way for me."

"I am here to help."

Barp!

"Until you've bled as much information from me as you can, grown frustrated when you realise I've been telling the truth about who I am, and then hand me back to Monica. This is the oldest routine in the book. One of you is nice after the other one's been horrible in an attempt to make me open up. To make me think you're on my side, even if Monica isn't. The teachers used to do it to us at school all the time."

"You went to school? Where are you from?"

"You're wasting your time." Max turned his face away from the cup of water. "I've told you all I know about this place."

But Gracie persisted and held the cup to his lips, tracking his head movements when he turned away from her again. He took a sip, his parched throat easing at the cold and wet massage.

"Who are you here with?" Gracie said.

What harm would it do to tell her most of the truth? "There's seven of us."

"What are your names?"

"I'm Max. The others are on the roof of the palace."

"What are their names?"

"Why do you want to know?"

"Just curious."

"Olga, Matilda, Cyrus, William, Hawk, and Artan."

"And this Olga's special, is she?"

The chains rattled above Max when he snapped his head back. "W-why do you say that?"

Barp!

Gracie shrugged and smiled. "You mentioned her first."

Heat spread through Max's cheeks. Were it not for the bulb next to his face, it might have been more obvious. Or maybe Gracie was just being polite.

Gracie said, "If what you've told us so far is the truth—"

"It is."

"Then when are your friends coming to let you out?"

If he told her where he'd put the key, he'd lose all his leverage.

"There are too many diseased in the wastelands at the moment. They're stuck on the roof of the palace."

"So how did you get over here?"

"I got lucky. I'm fast."

"I think there might be more to this story than you're letting on. How did you get in?"

Although Max opened his mouth, he had no words.

"Look," Gracie said, "your story doesn't add up. If you let yourself in, you need to have a key, and that key is somewhere. If your friends let you in, they need to come back and let you out at some point."

"I got in before the palace fell. Did you notice when the alarm stopped?"

"Of course."

Barp!

"Like I said to Monica, that's when the palace fell. I knew that because my friends had a plan to cut the electricity and let the diseased into the palace. That's what was going to kill Grandfather Jacks."

"So you don't know for certain whether he's dead or not?"

Max pressed his lips tight. The more he told her, the deeper he dug his hole.

"So ignoring where you've put the key, or when your friends are back, what are you doing in here?"

"I've come to break someone out."

"Not doing a very good job of that, are you?"

"I found her."

"You just weren't expecting Monica to use her as bait."

"What's Dianna ever done to Monica? She's an innocent girl from Umbriel."

"All of the women here are innocent, and half of them are from Umbriel. That's where you're from, is it?"

"We passed through there."

"On your way to …?"

"We don't know yet."

"What made you leave Umbriel?"

"They tried to kill us—"

"You and your friends on the roof of Grandfather Jacks' palace?"

"Yeah. They tried to kill us boys while they brought Olga and Matilda here."

"And they failed in their attempts?"

"Obviously."

"Remember who's tied up, Max." She looked him up and down as if to highlight the bonds holding him in place. "There could have been more of you. So you got Olga and Matilda out?"

"They got themselves out. We just caught up to them here."

"How come it's you breaking out Dianna and not one of the girls if they've managed to get free of Grandfather Jacks? That's no mean feat, you know."

Barp!

"Because I'm the one in the asylum."

"There's a lot you're not telling me."

"I could say the same for you. What's your deal? Monica seems batshit crazy, but from what I can tell, you're not."

"How can you tell?"

"Your words are reasoned. Your tone even."

"Hardly an expert diagnosis."

"It's the best I've got."

Gracie smiled and nodded. "Sometimes you have to pick sides. You asked me about those women and children who are still locked up. I picked a side, which means I'm not in a cell anymore. All I want is to get out of here. If you can help me do that, I can help you."

"I still don't trust you."

"I don't blame you. We don't know each other. But you know what they say about when you've hit rock bottom."

"There's only one way to go?"

Barp.

"So what do you have to lose in trusting me? You're in a world of shit right now; you might as well roll the dice."

"Do you know Dianna?"

"I was in the cell with her."

"Did you knock me out?"

Gracie shook her head. "That was Monica."

"Has Dianna sided with Monica?"

"She failed to see the possible opportunities of joining her gang. But she's alive, and I don't believe Monica will kill any of them. Although, she's not the easiest woman to make predictions on."

"Where's Dianna now?"

"In another cell."

"So what's your story?"

"I'm from a community farther south."

"South of the wall?"

Gracie laughed and shook her head. "No, of course not. You think I'd come back to this shithole if I was?"

Barp!

"How did you get here?"

"I was out hunting. I got separated from my hunting party, and I got jumped by a group calling themselves the Nomads."

"Scruffy bastards with bones in their hair and dreadlocks?"

"You've met them?"

"They're dead now."

"You're sure?"

"I watched them die. They also brought Olga and Matilda here. They were trying to keep us away from them."

For the first time, Gracie's shoulders slumped and she said, "They brought me here a few weeks back. I've been hoping my dad would have found me by now."

"Your dad's important?"

"We live in an underground community and he's the leader. He has a lot of people willing to do as he asks."

"How long are you going to wait for him to turn up?"

"Until today I didn't realise I had a choice. Hopefully I'll get out of here and I won't have to wait any longer. From talking to Monica, if you're too old to be on Grandfather Jacks' radar, you could be waiting in here a long time."

"No wonder she's lost the plot." Max said. "If I'd had to listen to that—"

Barp!

"—for most of my life, I'm not sure I'd be the full ticket either."

"But it looks like I might have a way out of this mess now," Gracie said.

"As long as Monica believes you're on her side."

"And we'll have to make sure she does, right?"

"What's stopping me telling her?"

"Your story has more holes in it than a fishing net. I'll keep my mouth shut if you do the same. I think we can help each other when the time's right. Maybe neither of us need to rely on Monica to get out of here."

"And you can help me get Dianna?"

"I can try."

CHAPTER 19

William stepped over the diseased's eyeless corpse after Olga. Tears of blood ran down its cheeks. "Why didn't the diseased in the arena bleed like the ones we've seen in the wild?"

"What are you talking about?" Olga said, her voice echoing as she entered the tight corridor.

"When we went to a main event in the arena back in Edin, the diseased didn't bleed like those in the wild. It was like their blood was congealed in their veins. I thought it was the same for all the diseased."

"They bleed them out," Artan said, stepping over the corpse and joining the others at the bottom of the stairs. "It makes them more docile. Easier to fight."

"How do you know that?" William said.

"It's the one useful thing my dad told me."

Maybe William should have asked that question sooner. "Before all this happened, going to a fight in the arena was the best. Now I feel like those days belonged to an entirely different person. Like I'm observing memories in which I played no part."

"None of us are those kids who went on national service," Olga said.

Around the bend, the small corridor's floor, walls, and ceiling were made from grey stone. Every surface glistened with damp, and the occasional drip of water fell from the hanging bulbs running down the centre of the ceiling. A door at the far end of the corridor, four more ran down the wall on their left.

Artan said, "Where do you think Hawk's go—"

Crash! It came from the first room on their left, the door open.

"That answer your question?" Olga said.

William went into the room first. He jumped aside as a splintered baton of wood hurtled towards him. As long as his forearm and several inches thick, it slammed into the wall on his right.

As Olga shoved her way in, William pushed her down, the *clang* of a steel bar flying over her head.

Hawk had a bat in his hand. A paddle of some sort, it looked like a torture device. While holding it in a two-handed grip, he took down the shelves along one wall, small clamps, gags, and thumbscrews tinkling when they hit the stone floor.

William slid the remaining chains from around his neck and threw them to one side. No wonder Hawk had been so distracted by them.

A stocks built for children sat in one corner. Tears glistened in Hawk's eyes and he grunted with the effort of his blows, hammering shots against the wooden frame.

At first it looked like the stocks wouldn't break. But Hawk redoubled his efforts, slamming blow after blow against it, faster and more furious with each attack.

The frame collapsed with a splintering crack.

His arms hanging down, his body rocking with his ragged breaths, Hawk left the room, barging William aside.

In the aftermath of Hawk's fury, the room trashed, Artan said, "So what do we do?"

"I think he needs to get this out of his system," Olga said.

"So we let him?" The *bang* of the door in the next room being kicked open, William pointed in the direction of the sound. "Have you heard how much noise he's making?"

"This is clearly important for him."

"What about what's important for Matilda?"

"We'll get her ointment, William. How can we possibly understand what Hawk's been through? I'm hoping this will be the catharsis he needs."

Into the next room first, William tried to piece together what it might have looked like before Hawk entered. A small table and chairs in one corner. A small bed in the other. Small leather masks and outfits hung on a rack above the bed. Hawk had used Cyrus' sword to tear holes in the leather and currently stabbed the mattress.

Tears streaked Hawk's cheeks, his teeth bared as he yelled a broken wail, cutting the mattress and duvet with his repeated attacks.

An outback hat hung over the back of one of the chairs. As Hawk picked it up, Olga said, "Grandfather Jacks used to wear them."

Hawk threw it on the bed, opened up the front of his trousers, and pissed on it, turning the worn brown leather limp.

William checked the corridor, poking his head from the room. It seemed clear. When he turned back, he nearly slammed into Hawk. "Uh …" William said, "I totally respect what you're going through, man."

Olga watched on with wide eyes.

"But will you please tell us when we get to the room

containing the ointment? And will you please make sure you don't destroy that too?"

An animalistic grunt, Hawk dipped his head and barged William aside, his strength damn near knocking William onto his arse. William couldn't leave Matilda's life to chance. He set off after him, but Olga grabbed him and pulled him back into the room. "Stay away from him. Let him do what he needs to."

"Even if that means sacrificing Matilda's life?"

A shake of her head, Olga said, "I don't think it will mean that."

"How can you be sure?"

"I can't, but—" her shoulders lifted with her wince at the crashing sound from the next room "—do you want to get in the way of that?"

They entered the room in time to see Hawk jump from a table and deliver a flying kick to a standing cupboard. A whip hung on the wall to William's left. The flayed leather end had glistening strips of razor-sharp metal woven through it.

The crashing and banging of Hawk destroying the room, William unhooked the whip and lifted it for the others to see.

Hawk yelled, raised a wooden chair above his head, and slammed it against the stone ground. Before he could kick over the other free-standing cupboard, the doors burst open and a diseased fell out. Stumbling at first, it turned left and right before snarling at Hawk.

But Hawk fixed on William rather than the creature. William, who stood in the doorway with the whip in his hand. The whip that had no doubt torn the scars into Hawk's torso.

Hawk charged and William froze. The furious hunter tore the whip from William's hand. Hawk ran back to the diseased.

A stinging throb on his right hand from where the razor metal had torn a gash in William's finger. What must it have been like as a boy to receive a lashing with that thing? The scars on Hawk's body said it all. And for those who needed a demonstration ...

The first crack of the whip tore a shred of the diseased's left cheek away. The creature's dark mouth spread wide as it screeched.

Another lashing, Hawk ripped a deep gash down the creature's chest. Like Hawk, the diseased stood topless.

Every time the whip cracked, the diseased yelled and cowered away. Several attacks later and the creature had fallen to the ground and curled into a ball. But Hawk continued tearing gashes into it. The weak light in the room cast deep shadows along Hawk's tense face. His next attack tore the skin on the creature's side, the cut so deep it exposed its ribcage.

Hawk screamed and cried. Snot and spittle sprayed away from him as he drove attack after attack into the creature. He'd torn its entire left side open, but he carried on, whipping until he'd shredded its arms.

By the time Hawk had finished, at least a third of the creature's skin had been flayed from its bones. The dead diseased lay in a pool of its own blood, glistening in the poorly lit room. Hawk spat on the thing and threw the whip down on top of it.

His attention on the ground, Hawk passed the other three on his way out.

"At least we now understand why he didn't want to come down here," Olga said. "Hopefully the ointment's in the next room."

CHAPTER 20

Monica's cackling laughter called from down the corridor, taking Max's words from him.

"If I were you," Gracie said, stepping several paces back, "I'd let her think you're a guard. At least then she'll have a reason to keep you alive. She'll believe someone will be coming for you at some point. You need to hold onto that power for as long as you can. It could be the difference between life and death."

Max's hands were numb, tingling streaks running down each of his forearms when he wriggled his fingers. "Surely you can let me out now? I can say I got out and overpowered you."

Gracie shook her head. "She won't believe that. Firstly, I'd kick your arse in a straight-up fight."

He breathed in through his nose and clamped his jaw to help him bite back his response. The steps of those outside got closer. "And second?"

"Where do you think Monica's just been? She's been in this place a long time and has a *lot* of friends. There's no chance she's coming back alone. We'd be taken down the second we tried to break out."

Barp!

Monica's cackle subsided and the footsteps closing in on the cell came towards them in stereo. How many more women did she have with her?

A final step away from Max, Gracie stood in the shadows as if she'd been there all along, a guard to watch over their prisoner, ready to report anything untoward to Monica.

The ratty woman in the dirty white top burst into the room and sneered at Gracie. "You get anything out of him?"

A shake of her head, Gracie said, "Nothing at all."

The footsteps that had joined Monica now took form as they entered the cell. They would have been hard to see were it not for the woman with the steel wheelbarrow filled with glowing coals. The deep orange light revealed the dirty faces of the ten or so women who now made up Monica's entourage.

With this many women around, Max had no chance of getting Gracie on her own again. But maybe she'd just shown him she could be trusted. After all, she'd spoken the truth about the extra inmates.

"This is the guard I was telling you about," Monica said.

One of the smaller women. In her mid to late twenties, she was almost as wide as she stood tall. Shaped like a ball, she rolled close to Max and dragged in a snotty sniff. "Sure smells like a guard."

"I've already told you," Max said, looking over the head of the short and round woman at her ratty leader, "I'm *not* a guard." Even though he didn't look directly at her, Max still caught Gracie's wince. And he definitely caught her words.

"Look at him," Gracie said, a twist to her features as mean as any of the women in the room with them. "You can tell he's lying."

"Why don't you go fuck yourself, G … you ginger bitch." Heat flushed his cheeks. Had Monica picked up on him nearly saying her name?

A slight twist of her head, Monica chewed on her bottom lip. She looked from Max to Gracie as if trying to read their connection.

Her eyes wide, Gracie retreated another step deeper into the shadows.

A long steel bar protruded from the hot coals in the barrow. Monica used it to stir the embers, sparks floating into the air and dying. The glowing end of the pole had more resilience. Bright orange, it lit up Monica's wicked grin.

The pins and needles in Max's arms buzzed so hard they damn near hummed. He worked his fingers, and while the movement radiated stinging streaks, the buzz eased.

The glow of the bulb close to Max's face had nothing on the tip of the steel bar. Monica brought it to within an inch of his left eye. The bar quietly hissed, and his skin itched as his pores released sweat.

"When will they be letting you out of here?" Monica said. "We need to get the hell out of this place, and you're our ticket to freedom."

"Which means you need to keep me alive."

"You can still be alive and in pain. I can make you wish you were dead."

Max's stomach lurched. What if he told Monica about Gracie now and how she said she'd help? Would it take the attention away from him? But if it did, what would it achieve? It wouldn't change the fact that Monica wanted information that he didn't have. He pressed his lips tight and shook his head. "I'm not a guard."

Gracie's head dropped.

Monica pushed the tip of the steel bar through Max's top covering his left pec. The smell of burned fabric gave way to the acrid stench of charred pork. The reek of his own seared flesh.

His jaw clamped, sweat running into his eyes, Max screamed, twisting and turning. The chains holding him in place rattled as the wooden baton swayed.

Although she'd looked at the floor, Gracie focused on Max again, her face twisting as if she experienced his pain. Like she had any fucking idea how he felt.

Monica might have pulled away, but his pec continued to burn as if she'd left the poker in his flesh. The insides of Max's thighs were damp with his own urine.

Barp!

"You either know where the key is to get out of here," Monica said, "or you have friends coming to get you. Which one is it?"

The moan leaving Max's lips sounded like it came from someone else. Febrile and grovelling, he whimpered as Monica pressed the fiery pole against the inside of his right thigh. Spasms ran up into his groin, and had he not already pissed himself, he would have lost control of his bladder at that point. The hiss of his own flesh mocked his struggles, joining Monica as she laughed harder than ever.

Gracie pressed her hands together, imploring him to give it up. Give Monica something. Maybe he should hand over the rat in her group? She wasn't doing him any good in that moment.

The swish of the coals in the barrow, more sparks kicked up from where Monica stirred them.

Trembling where he hung, his eyes stinging with sweat and tears, his breathing ragged, Max said, "I don't know when they're coming back for me."

A sudden halt. Some of the tension left Monica's back before she turned to face him. One eyebrow raised, a half smile revealed her top row of oversized yellow teeth. "I knew it! You are a guard." She handed the red-hot steel poker to the small round woman on her left. "He lied to me. Not that I should have expected anything less. The guards in this place are the lowest of the low. But at least you've told me the truth now. And at least we have a way out of here; we just don't know when. But we'll get that from you."

As Max shook his head, his restraints wobbled again, clattering and rattling. "Honestly, I don't know when they're coming."

Barp!

"I'll be the judge of that," Monica said.

"How can you be—"

"Burn his other thigh." Monica nudged the short fat woman in Max's direction. "Just to be sure he has nothing else to tell us."

"My pleasure," the woman said. "I hate the guards nearly as much as you do."

The hiss of the pole burned into Max's left thigh. He faced the ceiling and screamed so loud his throat burned nearly as much as his leg.

CHAPTER 21

As he'd done with every other room, Hawk charged off ahead of them and burst through the final door on the left side. Like with the others, it slammed against something inside the room with a *crack*! William walked on tired legs, and from the way both Olga and Artan maintained a walking pace and no more, they felt as exhausted. It had been a long few days with very little rest. When would it end? When would they—

A diseased screamed.

Olga led the charge, Artan next, William at the back, Jezebel raised. But he didn't need his axe.

The *tonk* of Hawk's boot slammed against skull from where he stamped repeatedly against the diseased's head.

Even now, after all they'd been through and seen, William's stomach spasmed when Hawk's final stamp crushed the diseased's cranium, his boot slamming down against the stone floor in a wet mush of brain matter and blood.

Where Hawk might have tried to hide it before, he now cried freely and spun full circle, taking in the room. It looked like a workshop. A large wooden bench on one side, a forge on the left of it, where they must have worked with steel.

While wiping his nose with the back of his sleeve, Hawk stopped turning. A large green curtain hung across a corner of the room. Other than Hawk's panting breaths, they stood in silence. Slow and deliberate steps towards the curtain, Hawk visibly trembled.

The *shing* of metal rings sang as they ran over the curtain rail. Seven boys aged from about six years old to about twelve rushed forward, slamming against the bars of their prison.

Small atrophied arms reached from the cage. Snapping jaws. Bleeding eyes. Several of them might have had cherub faces, but the horror of the disease stared from the soft surroundings. Their intent burned with cruelty.

Several seconds passed where Hawk shook his head. His words grew louder. "No, no, no, no, NO! After everything that's already happened to them." He stamped his foot.

All of the boys brandished the same scars as Hawk. Lashings around their neck. They'd all seen what that whip did to flesh. Although none of them had his rope burns.

"I can't take this," Hawk said, stepping away from the cage. "I can't take this anymore. I need to get out of here."

William pressed a hand into the centre of Hawk's sweating chest, halting his exit. "Wait."

Hawk shifted his weight from one foot to the other, his eyes roving as if to settle on anything in that room would invite madness.

"Just wait a moment," William said.

The *shing* of the curtain being closed made Hawk jump and raise his sword.

Olga lifted her hands in submission. "I'm sorry. I thought it was better closed. Now just hear William out."

"Look, Hawk, I can see how hard this is for you."

"What do you know?"

"I didn't say I understood. You're right. How could anyone possibly understand this unless they'd been through it themselves? I can see why you didn't want to come down here, and I'm so grateful you changed your mind. I recognise what this has taken from you, and it means a lot that you put yourself through this."

With every passing second, Hawk swayed more vigorously, hugging himself for warmth as he shifted his weight from his left foot to his right foot to his left foot.

"We've come this far," William said. "Can you please now show us where the ointment is for me to take back to Matilda? Please."

The darkness in Hawk's eyes lightened a little. He blinked repeatedly, his strong brow relaxing. His stare continued to move from left to right, not fixing on any one point. He looked at the ground as if he tried to find himself in the darkness of his mind. "Okay," he finally said. "Okay."

The room had a workbench and many cupboards. Hawk went straight for a small one in the corner and crouched down in front of it. The top of the clay pot rattled in his shaking grip when he placed it on the bench. He pulled the lid away and sniffed. For a moment, the darkness returned to his eyes, staining them like a burst of squid ink. "That's the stuff," he said. "I don't know what they make the ointment from, but it works every time. When I was younger, I saw some of the boys brought back from near death because Grandfather Jacks had beat them so severely."

The lid rattled again when Hawk replaced it, carrying the pot over to William. He gently placed the round clay container in William's hands. "I need to wait outside, so I need you to do me a favour."

William nodded. "Anything."

"Put those kids out of their misery. They've suffered

enough, and it's too dangerous to be leaving that many diseased alive down here."

The request sank through William and his throat dried, cutting off his words.

"Of course," Olga said, moving behind Hawk and ushering him out of the room. "You go and wait for us outside. We'll be out in a minute."

Before Hawk reached the door, his shoulders shook and he trembled. The back of his hand to his nose, he fell out into the hallway.

Her face ashen, Olga lifted her sword. "We have to do this for Hawk."

The stoic Artan turned even more so. A knife in each hand, he stepped closer to the cage.

Jezebel useless for what they needed to do, William walked over to the large wooden tool bench. A steel pole about three feet long and an inch thick. The end had been fashioned into a spike. Cold to touch and heavy in his grip, what had they planned to do with it? What did it matter? This room and everything in it now belonged to history.

Olga said, "Ready?"

Artan nodded. William shrugged.

Shing!

Olga ripped open the curtain and the diseased children rushed forward. All of them hit the bars head first, their prison completely invisible to them now they'd seen prey.

Several of the diseased fell back from their self-inflicted blows, but four of them remained pressed against the bars, reaching through.

While holding the steel pole in a two-handed grip, the wet *schlop* of Artan and Olga dropping diseased at his side, William moved closer to the boy directly in front of him. He had open wounds around his neck. They glistened with a white milky pus. What pain must he have been in before he turned? What pain must Matilda be in right now?

Close enough for the tips of the boy's fingers to scrape against his arms, William lined up the pole's spike, gripped the shaft tighter, and drove it into the boy's left eye.

The steel sank into the kid's face by half a foot, turning the creature limp. William tilted the pole so the kid slid backwards from it. Another life taken from this world far too soon.

CHAPTER 22

The short spherical woman came at Max again, the glowing end of her steel poker drawing traces in the air. At the winter solstice, all of Edin stayed up late and had small fires. They lit sticks so they glowed like the woman's pole, and they drew lines through the sky with them. Max always boasted he could spell his name before the traces from the first letter died. His brothers always humoured him. In truth, he couldn't even complete the *M* before the traces faded.

Wincing away from the approaching woman, Max jumped when Monica barked, "Stop!"

The short round woman must have heard her, but she kept coming.

"Sally, I said *stop!*"

Still Sally came forwards.

The tip of the pole shot up in the air, hit the low ceiling in the damp cell, and rained down a shower of sparks before it landed on the ground with a *clang!*

"What the fuck was that about?" Sally said.

Gracie had kicked the pole. She pulled her shoulders back

and leaned over the shorter woman. "Monica told you to stop."

And it might have escalated had the ratty Monica not stepped between the two. Ushering Sally back behind her, she looked Gracie up and down. "Taken a shine to him, have you?"

"Who likes seeing someone get burned?" Gracie said. "Maybe after I've spent years in this place, I might lose my empathy for others, but I've not been here long enough for that. I won't watch someone suffer unnecessarily."

"You'll do what I say!"

A tilt of her head to the side, Gracie showed she wouldn't.

Thankfully Max hadn't ratted her out. She'd help him when the time came. He had to trust her. Outing her to Monica wouldn't help any of them.

Monica's yellow teeth were so prominent it looked like she acted up to her rodent appearance. But if she did, she remained deadpan the entire time. "You must need a rest," she said.

The insides of Max's thighs and his left pec still burned as if the poker remained in them. He nodded, his voice weak. "Yes. Yes, I do."

"And you won't try any funny business?" Monica had to stand on a step beside Max to untie his right hand from the bar above him.

"Not at all," Max said. "I just want to get out of here."

The sting of pins and needles intensified as the blood rushed back down Max's arm. He opened and closed his right hand, balling it as he stared at Sally. She'd get hers soon enough.

His left hand now free, Monica stepped down from the box. "After all, we need to make sure you're ready for when the other guard comes and picks you up."

Max shrugged. "They're not going to open the door if they can't verify I'm okay."

"My thoughts exactly." Monica had left the ropes around Max's wrists. She tied them together, binding his hands behind his back. His feet still strapped in, she nudged him.

His stomach in his throat, Max fell forwards. Tugging on his bonds, he slammed down on the stone floor on both his knees. He yelled through clenched teeth. "Gargh!" But he managed to hold on to the barrage of expletives destined for Monica.

"Terribly sorry," Although her yellow-toothed smile and the glow of her black eyes didn't corroborate her sentiment. "I didn't mean to nudge you then. How are you, chick?"

Again, Max bit back his reply while Gracie lifted him to his feet.

"She really does like him, doesn't she?" Sally said.

But Monica didn't take the bait. Instead, she untied Max's ankles and allowed him to step from his bonds. The vicious woman grabbed the ropes around Max's wrists and nudged him forwards, guiding him from the cell into the corridor like a captured animal.

All the while, the same bone-juddering tone soared through the asylum's hallways. *Barp!*

"How long has it been since you've seen daylight?" Max said.

Fire tore through Max's back when Monica lifted his bound hands, forcing him forwards and onto his knees. She spoke in his left ear. Her hot breath made the skin at the base of his neck crawl. "Don't talk to me about my time in here. I'm feeling charitable at the moment. Any more of that nonsense and my goodwill will vanish."

Monica's entourage of eight to ten woman, including Gracie and Sally, walked behind them. Monica turned Max left and right, directing him where she wanted him to go.

They reached a ramp, which she guided him onto, leading him down a steep decline.

Every time Monica pushed Max a little too hard, his pulse spiked and another gush of sweat left him. His already burning wounds stung with the salty secretion. She then shoved so hard he tripped on the lumpy ground, his knees taking his fall for a third time.

Monica lifted Max up again by his bonds, the excruciating pain in his shoulder blades rivalling the burns on his chest and thighs. Her tone chipper, she said, "Whoopsie, clumsy clod. Come on, let's get you back on your feet."

At the bottom of the steep slope, Monica freed a bolt with a *clack* and opened a cell door. The hinges groaned. The bulb much weaker in this cell, Monica shoved Max in the back, sending him stumbling into the dark room.

The place reeked of damp. A few wobbly steps, Max found his way to a bed in the corner and sat before Monica could knock him down again. The mattress sodden, it instantly soaked his clothes.

"I'll let you rest now," Monica said, her entourage waiting in the hallway.

"Uh, do you have somewhere drier?"

"Oh, you have no idea."

Max frowned as she slammed the door shut, the bolt sliding home with a hard *crack*. What the hell did she mean by that? The sound of rushing water answered his question.

In a matter of seconds the floor had flooded, the water already an inch or two deep. Max's feet splashed as he ran through the shallow puddle to the door. He used his nose to trace the edges of the frame. The door had rubber seals running around it. Stepping back on wobbly legs, he said, "Shit, they're going to drown me."

CHAPTER 23

The water up to his chest, Max chased his panicked breaths. He couldn't swim. Especially with his hands bound behind his back. Instead of lubricating his bonds, the ropes around his wrists tightened. At least the cool water soothed his burns. Although, it soothed his burns while stealing the air from his lungs.

Snap! The hatch in the door opened. Higher than most, Max had to look up to see through it.

"If you were a guard, you would have known about this room. So tell me the truth and we might be able to find a way out of there for you. Where is the key to get out of this place?"

The glow from the hallway outside showed Monica's ratty face. She must have been standing on a platform of some sort.

"Come on, Max," Monica said. "Time's running out in there. If you tell me the truth, it'll be easier for all of us."

"You'll let me go?"

"I'm certainly more inclined to if you show me the key."

"But—"

"Look at it this way, Max. You've seen what I'm prepared to do to you. Now, I know you know where the key is, but if you don't give it up, what use are you to me?"

The water had now reached Max's chin. It splashed when he shook his head. "But that key's the only thing keeping me alive."

"*I'm* the only thing keeping you alive, and trust me, my mood can change like the weather. Do you want to feel the full force of my thunderstorm?"

"Okay," Max said, shivering as cold and adrenaline coursed through him.

"Okay?" Her tone playful, Monica said, "I know you're under pressure in there, Max, but you need to be slightly more articulate than that."

"I'll show you where the key is to get out of here."

Snap! The hatch shut and Monica's voice echoed in the hall outside. "Drain the cell."

The rushing water halted and Max let go of a hard exhale. Thank the stars. Although, what had he just done? He'd given up his only advantage.

CHAPTER 24

Whether exhaustion or shock, something sent a violent tremble through William when he left the room containing the previously infected, now dead boys. Flecks of their blood covered his clothes, and he relived the sensation of driving the pole's tip into their bodies.

Her skin pale, her eyes bloodshot, Olga looked one way and then the other. "Where's Hawk?"

Artan shook like he had hypothermia, his two blades hanging from each hand. They dripped with the boys' blood.

"What must Hawk have gone through at the hands of Grandfather Jacks?" Olga said.

William sighed. "No wonder he's abrasive sometimes."

One sharp shake of her head, Olga spoke through gritted teeth. "I wish I'd had more time to kill him. I would have peeled the skin from his back an inch at a time."

"It wouldn't have made any difference." Artan laid a hand on Olga's right shoulder. "The damage is done. You've prevented him inflicting any more pain on anyone else. You should celebrate that."

"Hardly seems like a time for celebration."

"Just know you've done a good thing for this world by ending him."

William inhaled through his nose, his chest rising with the intake. "I fear his effects will stay with many of the people who came into contact with him for the rest of their lives."

"Did you see the scars around Hawk's neck?" Artan said.

"It's hard to miss them," Olga said.

"I mean the rope burns. He said Dianna found him and kept him alive. Maybe he's gone to repay the favour?"

The clay pot cool in his hands, William raised it, the liquid swirling inside. "Hawk did well to hold it together long enough to help us get this. We need to get it back to Matilda."

"But what do we do about Hawk?" Olga said.

"He's chosen not to wait for us."

Old hinges groaned and the door at the end of the corridor that they'd yet to go through swung out towards them, driven wide by a gentle draft. It looked like the entrance to a mine. About seven feet tall and four feet wide, the only way through it would be in single file.

Barp! The tone called at them from the depths of the tunnel. The weak lighting did little to reveal what lurked inside.

Artan picked up some wooden splinters before he let them fall again. "At least we know where Hawk has gone. Look …" He pulled the door towards him. A map had been drawn on the other side of it. A map of the asylum.

William's jaw fell loose and he shook his head. "The place looks like a maze."

"So what do we do?" Artan said. "Do we follow him?"

"He might have been hard to be around, but he helped us in every way he could," Olga said. "He probably needs us like we needed him. I'd imagine if he had people around, he'd feel a lot better."

"But he chose to leave us here," William said. "If that doesn't tell you he wants to be left alone, then I don't know what does. And I have to go to Matilda. She's already waited too long to get this." He lifted the cool clay pot again. "I understand you might want to go back to Hawk, so if I have to return to Matilda on my own, I will. But I can't leave her any longer. I'm sorry."

"You're right," Olga said. "It might be a wild-goose chase to follow Hawk. Let's get back to Matilda first and then maybe look for Hawk after."

"Okay." William waited for Artan's nod. "Let's go." As he led them back down the corridor towards the stairs out of there, he said, "Now we need to hope this ointment is as good as Hawk says it is."

CHAPTER 25

Even after all this time in the asylum, or maybe especially after all this time, the *barp* shaking the damp stone walls twisted through Max, and he tugged against his bonds as he walked down the dark stone corridor. His clothes sodden, they pressed against the burns on his chest and the insides of his thighs. His wrists sore from where the ropes dug in, the sharp sting served as a potent reminder that he couldn't get free. If only he had something to cover his damn ears.

Monica beside him, her gang of about ten women surrounded them, including the toxic Sally. Max walked with slow and deliberate steps, his knees still throbbing from taking the brunt of several falls.

"Are you going to speed this up?" Monica said.

"I can't see very well."

When Sally shoved Max in the back, he half-tripped, stumbling forwards, his stomach lurching in anticipation of yet another fall.

"Sally," Monica hissed, "stop it!"

"He answered you back."

"Did I ask you to stick up for me?"

Sally mumbled her way into silence.

Gracie close by. At least, she had been close by. Hard to tell in the deep shadows. Many of the other women held back as if they wanted no part in Monica's madness. But better to be outside a cell than in it, right?

The conversation with Sally had sharpened Monica's words. "And you're sure you know where you're going?"

The line of bulbs stretching away from them along the dark and damp corridor forced Max to squint. "I think so."

"You *think* so?"

"Shut *up,* Sally. You think so?" Monica said.

"Look," Max said, halting beside a screaming woman in a cell on their right, her arms reaching from the barred window, "we've already established I'm not a guard. This place is like a damn maze, so if it takes me a little longer to find my way, you're going to have to be patient."

"Don't tell me what I'm going to have to be. Also, I don't do very well with being patient."

"I'm trying my best, Monica."

Sally leaned close to Max, her halitosis breath in his ear. "Your best isn't good enough."

"Is the key near the entrance?" Monica said.

"Why would I hide it there?"

Sally shoved Max again. He ran on the edge of his balance, trying to get ahead of his fall. But he tripped, stumbled, and landed on his knees on the stone floor. Her boot narrowly missed his face from where Monica pulled her away before she could kick him in the head. She shoved her back to be with the other women. The group wrapped around her, several of them holding her back.

While helping him to his feet, Monica said, "You need to

be careful, Max. There's a way to talk to me and you're straying very far from it."

More streaking pains running down the front of his legs, Max moved off again with a limp.

They turned around several corners, the same *barp* going off again and again. Crazed screams from all around them. Children crying. "Monica?"

The woman spun on him, her eyes wide, her face taut.

"You said you've been here a long time," Max said. "So you know what the kids are going through. Why don't you let them out?"

"What's that got to do with me being here for a long time?"

"You know what time in this place does to someone. You can stop the kids having to suffer like you have."

Monica licked her lips, her brow furrowed, her chest rising and falling. Although the tight wind to her narrow shoulders suggested she wanted to let rip, instead she said, "I have plans to let them out. Of course I do. But I need to get control of the asylum first. I can't let chaos into the corridors if we're all trapped. So the sooner you show us the way out, the sooner we can free the children."

"But what harm will kids do?"

"Have I asked you for your advice?"

Max stepped away from her reach before continuing down another long corridor that looked exactly like all the others.

"All I want from you is the key to get out of here. If you're lucky, I'll let you live after that, but don't bank on it."

A voice hissed from the darkness, "Don't bank on it at all."

"Shut up, Sally," Monica said. "Now, Max, show me where the key is before I cut your throat."

The tap of their heels along the stone floor filled what

little silence this place gave them as they continued walking. "Where were you from before this?" Max said.

Max winced when Monica's eyes glazed. His knees still throbbed. Several women on either side of them reached out into the hallway. "Sister, let us out."

If Monica heard them, she hid it well. "I was lost with my family in the wastelands."

A quickening of his pulse, Max let her speak. "Grandfather Jacks took us in and promised to help us." Her eyes filled with tears. "That was the last time I saw daylight."

"What happened to your family?"

Monica moved so quickly, Max didn't see her coming. In his face, eyeball to eyeball, she forced him back several stumbling steps until he slammed against a cell door behind him with a *crash!* An arm reached through the window. Thick like a constrictor, it caught him around his throat and tightened.

Gritting his teeth against the stinging rope burns on his wrists, Max tugged against his bonds in an attempt to get free. For what good it did. As he gasped, stars swimming in his vision, he worked his jaw, digging his chin into the forearm choking him. But they held on. He kicked the door behind like a horse in a stable.

Her pointing finger close to his right eyeball, Monica bared her teeth, the whites of her eyes wide. "How the hell do I know what's happened to my family?"

His gasping breaths drowned out by the loud tone. The already dark corridors grew darker. Max's pulse swelled through his temples as if his head might pop, and he could only manage to mime the words, *Help me. Help me.*

Gracie appeared in the light cast by the bulbs closest to Max. A knife in her hand, which she'd pulled from Monica's belt, she jabbed the tip into the elbow of the arm across Max's throat.

The arm slithered back into the dark cell, the thick hand catching one of the bars with a *whack!*

Max fell forwards. He landed on his knees again, panting and gasping, his throat still locked tight as if the arm still had a grip on him.

Before Max could catch his breath, Monica pulled him to his feet by his bonds. His shoulder blades bending farther than they had any right to, he stood up on one knee and then the next.

As Max stood, Monica leaned close to his right ear. "Now find that key before I lose my shit. I'm going to count down from one hundred, and if we're no closer to finding it, I'm going to cut your throat. One hundred … ninety—"

Barp!

Max shoulder-barged Monica aside, sending her slamming into the door of a cell with a crash before she fell into a crumpled heap.

Sally came forwards like an octopus. All limbs, the short fat woman released a shrill cry.

A tight clench to his jaw, Max bent his legs to test the spring in his knees before he jumped straight up and kicked her in the face. The blow connected with a *schlop,* a spray of spittle flying up away from her mouth, her feet running ahead of her while the upper half of her body went back. She landed on the stone floor with a hollow bark.

Before Sally got up, Max charged her. "You fucking arsehole." He kicked her so hard it hurt his foot.

Despite the strength of his blow, Sally remained conscious, twisting and turning on the ground.

Max lifted his boot over her head, clamped his jaw, and stamped. Something cracked. The skin at the back of his knees tingled as if his legs might give out.

Sally had now turned well and truly limp.

While Monica got to her feet, Max backed towards Gracie. "Cut me free, please. This is the best chance we have."

Gracie slid the knife into his bonds and cut the ropes.

Max caught Monica with a right cross to the chin, sending her back against the wooden door and dropping her for a second time. While reaching out to Gracie, he said, "Come on, let's get out of here."

CHAPTER 26

William led Olga and Artan away from the door Hawk had vanished through, down the dingy corridor in the direction of the stairs leading to the ground floor of the palace. With everything that had gone on, he'd forgotten about the diseased Hawk had killed until he turned the corner. The tears of blood had now dried. The mouth remained open in a silent scream.

"Bloody hell," Artan said. "Maybe it's for the best he's gone off on his own. I'm not sure how many times I could watch his way of killing the diseased."

"He's had a hard time of it," Olga said.

Fatigue thickened William's blood, and the ascent up the stone stairs sapped his energy. By the time he'd reached the top, his legs trembled and sweat dampened his brow. He breathed in heavy pants, the lid on the ceramic pot rattling in his shaking grip.

Slipping his knives into his belt, Artan untied the chains holding the doors closed and stepped aside.

Jezebel in one hand, the ceramic pot in the other, William nudged the doors with the toe of his right boot, but before he could push them wide, Olga pulled him back. "What is it?" he said.

"Give me the ointment. You can't fight with only one hand free."

William pulled the clay pot into his chest. "No offence, but we've done a lot to get this. I can't give it to anyone else."

"Fine," Olga said. She tossed her sword so it flipped in the air, and caught it by its tip, offering the handle to William. "Take this and give me Jezebel."

When William paused, Olga tilted her head. "Don't tell me you can use that axe one handed? At least you have some chance with my sword."

William handed the clay pot over. "Take care of it, okay?"

"Obviously." Olga rolled her eyes and shook her head as she gripped the clay pot with one hand and held her sword with the other.

"You ready?" William said.

"I'm not sure it's us you need to be asking," Olga said.

"Fine." William waited for Artan's nod. "On my count. Three, two, one …" Right until that moment William had expected himself to be cautious. To push the door open slowly to see what waited for them in the hallway. But something changed during the countdown, adrenaline flooding his system, driving him forwards as he kicked the doors wide and charged out with Jezebel raised above his head.

Artan and Olga on his heels, the muscles in William's arms twitched from where he kept Jezebel raised. He looked one way and then the other. "Huh?"

"Where the hell are they?" Olga said.

Barp!

Daylight shone down the corridor from one end. Olga peered that way, standing on her tiptoes as if it would somehow allow her to see through walls. "Looks like that noise works, then. I'm guessing they've all gone to the asylum. I didn't …"

Although Olga continued talking, William stopped hearing her. He stumbled towards Grandfather Jacks' comfort room. The chain he'd tied around the handles now lay on the floor. It had been untied and discarded.

Artan's face ashen, the knives in both of his hands twitched. "You think someone has been through here since we went into the basement?"

"It seems like the only logical conclusion."

"That doesn't mean it's the correct one," Olga said.

Artan shrugged. "You have another explanation?"

"No."

"So what's your point?"

"We need to be ready to fight," Olga said, "but there's no point in fighting enemies in our heads. We need to be prepared, but standing in this hallway talking about what might be on the other side of this door won't give us any answers. Chains aren't the easiest things to tie knots in. Maybe a diseased knocked it off?"

She made sense. They at least needed to see what waited for them inside the comfort room. Without the countdown this time, William hit the button beside the door three times and entered with Jezebel raised.

The four diseased they'd dropped on their way in remained on the floor. Their blood had pooled around them. Sallow cheeks and dry crusty eyes. "If this is all we have to deal with," Artan said, "then that's fine by me." A breeze ran through the room until Olga hit the button three times to close the door behind her. "But did we leave the window open?"

William shrugged. "I don't remember closing it." His palms sweating, his heart in his throat, his mouth dry, he pulled in a long breath through his nose. "Like Olga said, we can only deal with what we can see."

Artan moved like a lizard. One step on the small table by the window, he slipped outside and pulled himself up, his boots vanishing from sight before he called down, "All clear."

William took the ointment from Olga, who went out of the window next.

The small table wobbled when William stood on it, a surge of panic quickening his pulse before he sat on the window ledge. Blinded for a few seconds by the bright midday sun, tiredness and sweat added to the burn in his eyes. He handed the clay pot to Olga, who took it and placed it on the roof before she leaned down to take Jezebel.

But before William could hand over his weapon, two hands wrapped around his ankles. A tight grip on each, they tugged hard, yanking him away from his friends. The rough window ledge tore fire up his back and he whacked his head. A tone like a struck bell rang in his ears as he lost sight of the blue sky and Olga staring down on him.

CHAPTER 27

Max dragged Gracie away from the downed Monica. His punch had knocked her backwards, and she slammed her head on the wall behind her. She currently lay slumped on the floor. The only head start they'd get, they had to make it count.

The tone continued unrelenting and with metronomic regularity. It timed their escape and how long it would be before they were caught. It mocked their efforts. Did they really think they could get away from Monica? Were they really that naïve?

More screams and cries, almost as if every inmate had tuned into Max's galloping pulse. As if they were invigorated by the thrill of the chase.

Each long and shadowy corridor looked like the next and the previous. The first chance Max got, he turned right, dragging Gracie with him as he tore down a corridor exactly the same as the one they'd left behind.

His steps clumsy, his breathing heavy. His damp clothes rubbed against his burns. Whatever happened, at least Sally had gotten hers. The toxic bitch deserved to be taken out.

Still holding hands with Gracie, their grip sweaty, Max took them down a sharp left.

"Do you know where you're going?" Gracie said.

Max slowed down and listened to the asylum.

Barp!

The same shrieks and cries from the inmates. They were enraged circus animals on a full moon. Tormented by their incarceration, when those doors opened, they'd come flooding out as the personification of madness.

"First," Max said, "we lose them."

"And then?" Gracie's face glistened with sweat.

"Then we get out of here." But he didn't set off.

Gracie looked back over her shoulder. "What are you waiting for?"

"What if we opened the cell doors now? We'd be much harder to find if we let this insanity out into the hallways."

"You're probably the only man in this place," Gracie said. "You'll stand out like a beacon, even in the relative darkness. You have the key hidden somewhere, right?"

"Of course I do," Max said.

Barp!

The thunder of footsteps came towards them. Max took off and Gracie followed. They were fast. They could outrun Monica and her crew.

Another sharp left and then another right. Every corridor made from the same dark grey stone. The same smells of dirt and human waste in the air. The same uneven ground. But with so many twists and turns, it meant the building took the echoes of their slamming steps and scattered them to the four corners of the compass. It would have sounded like they made several different escapes, so which one would Monica and her band of women follow? A group that small could only split so many ways.

Several twists and turns later, Gracie pulled on Max's

right shoulder, slowing him to a halt. A few seconds passed where she leaned forwards and rested her hands on her knees, her mouth wide, her long plait hanging down in front of her face.

All the while, Max clenched his jaw against the buzzing sting in his burns, the unrelenting throb burrowing deeper into his body like three white-hot worms.

"I think we've lost them," Gracie finally said. "We need to get out of here before it's too late."

He had to admit it sooner or later. Stepping back a pace, Max winced when he said, "How well do you know this place?"

Barp!

The poor light cast grotesque shadows across Gracie's twisted face. "You don't know the way out of here? What the fuck, Max? We just … *You* just killed someone back there."

"I'm sorry—"

"Sorry doesn't cut it."

"This place is a maze."

"You're only just realising that now?"

"No, it's just—"

The flush of exertion gave way to a glow of fury. Gracie stepped close to Max, her face inches from his. She radiated heat. "It's just what? What possible excuse is there for you putting my life in this much danger?"

Bang!

Someone kicked the door of the cell on their right. A child cried while skinny arms reached out for them. "Please," the woman said, "please let us out of here. We've been in this place for so long. We just want to be free. We won't cause any trouble."

The urge to open their cell twitched through Max's right hand, his fingers tensing and relaxing. But like Gracie had said, as the only man in the place, he'd stand out from a mile away. Not only the only man in the place, but the only person who knew the location of the key to get them out of there. Things would turn sour very fast.

"Come on." Max pulled on Gracie's hand, leading her away. "We definitely won't get out if we stand here arguing. Let's go."

CHAPTER 28

Thankfully William had given Olga the ointment first. Not much he would have been able to do armed with a clay pot of liquid he didn't want to spill while his battle axe lay on the roof of the palace.

The boy must have been three to four years younger than William. Topless and covered in scars, his dirty face locked with a twist of pure hatred. He held a steel bar with both hands and brought it crashing down.

Clang! William lifted Jezebel's handle, blocking the blow.

The boy threw another two-handed attack, and William blocked it a second time, deflecting the steel pole. An inch closer to his right hand and the boy would have shattered his fingers.

William rocked forwards, sat up, and drove the end of Jezebel's handle into the boy's face. He connected with his nose with a deep *crunch!*

As the boy stumbled backwards, his wide eyes watering, William threw a kick at his hand. He dropped the pole with a *clang!*

The boy came at William with swinging fists, blood pouring from his nose.

Ducking one attack and jumping back from another, William used the end of Jezebel's handle again. This time he caught the kid's cheek. "Why are you trying to fight me?"

Even with what must have been a broken nose, partly blinded by his own watering eyes, and a welt growing on his cheek, the boy yelled and charged. He hadn't come here for a conversation.

William kicked the boy in the chest. He hit him so hard, the boy stumbled backwards. His arms flew wide when he tripped on one of the downed diseased and fell back into the wardrobe, the doors now open from where he must have burst from it. The boy slammed into the back wall with a *crunch!*

Heavy breaths rocked through William and he wiped his damp brow. "Are you finally done? I really don't want to have to kill you."

The boy didn't reply.

"Are you operating on your own?"

The boy still didn't reply.

"What's going on? Who are you here with? Why did you attack me?"

At that moment, Olga landed in the room, her feet hitting the stone ground. "Uh, William, I think he's dead."

"Huh?"

The boy's mouth hung open and his eyes were glazed. His ragged breathing had stopped. He stood motionless in the wardrobe, his arms hanging by his sides. Blood leaked from his nose and dripped from his chin. Pegs ran along the back of the wardrobe. Each one about four inches long and half an inch in diameter, they pointed upwards from the back wall. One of the pegs had entered his skull through the soft part at the back.

To be sure, William slipped two fingers along the kid's still-warm neck. They came back coated in blood. "No pulse. Shit!"

Olga pushed William aside and closed the wardrobe's doors. "He shouldn't have come at you. There was no need for that. He made a choice, and you had to defend yourself."

A lump swelled in William's dry throat. Gulping did little to soothe it. "He was only a kid."

"I saw. But he attacked you. The more important question is, are there any more of them?"

"I hope not." William stepped over the four diseased corpses on his way back to the window. "We need to get up to Matilda and Cyrus to check."

A slight nod, Olga said, "I think so too." She clapped a hand on his shoulder. "Come on, let's go."

CHAPTER 29

Back on the roof, the tiles uneven, the pitch sloping down to William's right. A low-level buzz of fatigue ran through his limbs. Olga walked beside him, Artan higher up beside her.

Barp!

The wind dried William's sweat and he shivered. The asylum stood resolute. "It's so close."

"But with that many diseased between us and it, Max is still on his own," Olga said.

Artan said, "How long do you think it'll take for all the diseased to go around the front?"

Olga shook her head. "Too long."

Cyrus waved when they crested the next peak in the roof. "Where's Matilda?" William said. He quickened his pace. "Where's—" She sat on the roof holding her thigh. He jogged over to her with the clay pot. "You're okay?"

"Of course I'm okay." Matilda winced, the same pale and glistening sheen to her skin. "But please tell me you found the ointment?"

William held up the pot.

"Where's Hawk?"

While sitting down beside her and untying her bandage, William said, "He's still in there. We found a tunnel leading to the asylum. He went down it."

The wind made the dirty bandages flap while William exposed the deep cut on Matilda's thigh. A layer of milky pus covered it. His hands filthy and coated with dried blood from the boys in the cage and the one in the wardrobe, he handed Matilda the pot.

Although she took it, she stared at his hands.

"It's a long story. But I think it's best you do it. I don't want to rub more infection into your wound."

Matilda lifted the lid and poured the brown gloopy ointment. When it landed in the gash, she drew a sharp breath. The wound about an inch deep, the liquid filled it and shimmered, her leg trembling.

"How does it feel?" William said.

"It burns."

"Shit."

"But in a good way. I think it's supposed to burn."

The others watched on before Olga nudged Cyrus forward. "You need to put some on your hand too."

The boy still held onto the steel guardrail they'd given him when they left. He crouched down in front of Matilda and held his hand out.

Like Matilda had, Cyrus pulled in a sharp breath, gritting his teeth against the clear burn from the ointment.

The glazed eyes of the boy in the cupboard stared at William in his mind's eye. "Have you two seen anyone up here?"

"No." Cyrus shook his head. "Are there more survivors?"

After sharing a glance with Olga, William sighed and his shoulders sagged. "We don't know."

"What's happened?" Matilda reached over and held William's hand.

"We ran into a boy inside who attacked me."

"And now he's …?"

William pressed his lips together and shrugged. "I tried." His voice strained through the lump in his throat, he added, "It was him or me."

Matilda squeezed a little bit harder. "Well, I'm grateful for the outcome, then."

"Hey!" William said. Artan and Olga had walked away from the group. "Where are you two going?"

The sun in her eyes, Olga squinted when she looked back, the wind tossing her hair. "There are still two of us in there. We're going back in to find Hawk and Max. Hopefully Max has already found Dianna. We need to show him there's another way back. He might be able to cross the meadow, but she can't."

Still holding Matilda's hand, William said, "Can't we wait a little bit longer?"

"You don't have to come," Olga said. "Why don't you stay and rest? Be with Matilda for a while. You've spent a long time apart. Artan and I will be okay."

But he couldn't let them go on their own. If they didn't make it back and he'd waited on the roof with Matilda, he'd never forgive himself. A damp weight in his chest, William hooked the thumb of his free hand over his shoulder. "I need to—"

"I know." Matilda smiled, her brown eyes glistening. "You've done all you can for me and Cyrus. The others need you more right now. Just make sure you come back, okay?"

"Of course." William leaned forwards and kissed Matilda. He lingered with their lips touching before pulling away and filling his lungs. If he didn't leave her now, he never would. Artan and Olga had continued to walk away. Maybe they sensed his hesitance and wanted to give him every opportunity to stay. "I love you, Tilly."

Her smile stretched wider. "And I you. Now go!"

His fatigue no better for the shortest of rests, William got up on wobbly legs and ran after his friends. Max and Hawk needed them the most right now.

CHAPTER 30

"We will find our way out of here," Max said, "I promise."

"Unless your promises are made from maps, I'm not sure they're worth anything."

And she had a point. Max had coerced Gracie into helping him, and he'd now well and truly let her down. How the hell would he find their way out of this place?

"I've put my life on the line for you."

"I know." His breathing came in gasping waves, and his face twisted against the pain of his burns. He nodded, his voice growing weak. "I know."

Barp!

His legs leaden, his steps heavy, each one falling into the next, Max said, "At least there are only about ten of them. With the screams from the other prisoners, that damn tone running through the place, and the seemingly infinite choices of which way to turn, surely we can lose them? How hard can it be?"

"That's all well and good, but if we can't get out of here, what does it matter if we lose them?"

"We'll find a way out eventually."

Another lull in the chaos, the shrill scream of an enraged Monica filled it. Several corridors away, she shouted, "I'm going to let you all out. The first one of you—"

Barp!

Max screwed his face up as if it would help him hear better.

"—the boy," Monica continued, "gets their freedom."

"What's she saying?" Gracie said.

Monica shouted again. "The boy has the key to get us all out of here."

Gracie let go of a hard exhale. "So much for their only being about ten of them. Shit!"

The next turn Max took led them up a ramp similar to the one that had taken them down to the room that flooded. It took them farther away from Monica's madness, but they had no chance of making an escape if they were on the wrong floor. "Do you have any idea where Monica's keeping Dianna?"

"No. And I think we should focus on getting ourselves out of here first," Gracie said. "What use are we to Dianna if we're dead?"

The corridors stretched for what felt like miles. It didn't matter how many left or right turns Max took, every hallway looked the same as the last. Miles of corridors, miles of cells housing insanity. Miles of withered arms reaching out to them for salvation. Although would daylight emancipate their minds, or would it shine a spotlight on their torment? How many women were like Monica in this place? How many had been locked away years ago and left to rot?

The slope of the next turn caught Max off guard and he nearly fell, his run accelerated by the steep decline. The flagstones uneven, his toes caught raised lumps, his pulse spiking in anticipation of a fall. His arms thrust out for balance, he stumbled several more times but managed to remain on his feet.

Just as they got to the bottom of the slope, Gracie caught up to Max and dragged him back.

Barp!

A crowd of women and children at least fifteen strong raced along the corridor in front of them.

Leaning so close her words tickled Max's ear, Gracie breathed heavily and said, "I think that's all of them for now."

"Thank you." Max nodded and ran out into the corridor.

The *crack* of freeing bolts called through the asylum. Not only had Monica taken to opening the cell doors, but all the other women had too. The freeing of the prisoners spread like the disease, starting small and growing exponentially.

The echoes of liberation swirled through the place. They were everywhere.

Another left and right, Max came to an abrupt halt, Gracie slamming into his back.

As he turned full circle, his eyes stinging from trying to see in the gloomy corridors, his burns almost audible with their fierce buzzing, Max said, "I recognise where we are."

"It looks like every other corridor we've been in."

The cells in this part of the asylum were still locked. Max walked over to a closed door and peered into the shadows.

When the woman's face sprang up on the other side, he gasped and stepped back into Gracie, who shoved him in response. "You stood on my toe."

"S-sorry." But it was her. The same matted hair. The same sores on her face. The same missing teeth. "Gracie, this woman showed me the way out last time. We're close to the exit. Hi." Max waved at the woman.

"You're back," the woman said.

When the loud tone subsided, the *crack* of bolts being

freed sang through the long and dark corridors. "They're letting everyone out," Max said.

But the woman shook her head. "Don't open this door."

"Which way do I need to go to get out of here?"

Her pale arm no more than bones sheathed with skin, several sores dotted along it, the woman pointed.

"We can't go that way," Gracie said.

The cracks of freeing doors confirmed it. Monica and the inmates were getting closer, coming towards them from the direction the woman pointed. "Shit."

The opening bolts also came from the other way. They were closing in from both sides. Max said, "Maybe we need to make a break for it anyway? They're coming no matter which way we run."

It started low like a distant tsunami, but the sound quickly grew. The thunder of steps drawing nearer. A scream of liberation. A tide of freed prisoners.

Gracie shook her head, looking one way and then the other. "We have no chance getting past that lot."

The woman in the cell pointed with her bony finger to the cell opposite. She leaned so close to the bars in the door, they squashed her cheeks. Her black hair as matted and greasy as any prisoner Max had met, her dirty stench caught in the back of his throat. The woman spoke in a quiet voice as if she didn't want the women in the cell behind to hear. "That one's empty. Why don't you hide in there? If they're looking for you, I can't imagine they'll search the cells."

Gracie shook her head. "I don't like it."

"Do you have a better suggestion? It might be a good place to lie low."

"You sound like you've made up your mind."

"I'm happy to have it changed."

The rush of people drew closer, and Max bounced on the

spot, desperate to spend the nervous energy running through him. "Come on, Gracie, you need to make a decision now."

Her long ginger plait flicked one way and then the other with her turning head. She clearly had nothing. But Max let her come to the conclusion herself, the stampede closing in from every angle.

"Damn it!" Gracie led the way, darting into the dark cell on the other side of the corridor.

She let Max in and tried to close the door behind him, but he grabbed her arm and spoke in a low voice. "Leave it open. We want them to think it's empty."

They moved to the back of the cell and leaned against the cold and damp wall. Both of them panted from their run, and Max's throat had turned dry. He reached down and held Gracie's sweating hand as the charge of liberated prisoners flashed past in front of them. "Thank you for helping me."

"You could have ratted me out to Monica and you didn't," Gracie said. "I knew from that point that I could trust you. Although, had I known we'd end up here, I'm not sure I would have been on board. I thought you had a better plan."

"So did I. I'm sorry. We'll get out of here." More people streamed past the open cell. "I promise."

"I hope so," Gracie said. "I really hope so."

CHAPTER 31

Barp!
Of course the hinges groaned on the wooden door leading from the palace's basement to the tunnel connected to the asylum. They cackled like an old crow, a prophet of doom, appalled at even the notion that William, Olga, and Artan were about to enter the place.

The dark tunnel had bulbs lighting the way, but they were more spaced out than any of the bulbs anywhere else in the palace. More shadow than light, William's legs were tense with reluctance and his throat locked tight.

Olga must have picked up on it. Slapping his back, she said, "We can only fight what we can see. I know I've said it already, but I can't hear any diseased, and while I'm going to be ready should any turn up, we can't beat ourselves before we've taken a look. Also, what other routes are there to get to Max?" She shoved past William and took the lead into the shadowy tunnel.

"Anyway," Artan said, flicking his head at the door on their left, the room where they found the diseased boys who had once belonged to Grandfather Jacks, "I don't know about you, but anything has to be better than standing next to this room for any longer."

Barp!

As Artan followed Olga into the darkness, William walked forwards in his mind several times, but his limbs were locked so rigid, it felt like rigor mortis.

The tunnel had a curve, which Olga vanished around. Her voice echoed off the tight walls. "Go back to Matilda if you like. We won't hold it against you."

After all Max had done for them, William couldn't leave him. Matilda and Cyrus would be okay on the roof of the palace. How could he even think about not following the others?

Like every journey, this one started with the first step. The crossing of the threshold into the dank tunnel. It looked like it had been built long before the palace or the asylum. Gloomy, rich with the earthy tang of damp, the floors and walls uneven. William pushed on.

Barp!

William quickened his pace, but stopped almost instantly when he rounded the bend. Olga and Artan had halted in front of a small steel door. It hung open, an inch of light glowing in the crack surrounding it, shining out into the darkness of the tunnel. Olga had her hand resting on the door as if about to push it wide. Artan stood behind her, a slight bend to his legs from where he stood ready to fight, his knives held out in front of him. Whatever came their way, they'd deal with it.

Maybe William had made himself the passenger on this journey already. Freezing before the tunnel had shown he didn't want to take action. Olga and Artan didn't seek his advice, Olga shoving the door wide, light flooding into the dank corridor.

The pair of them rushed in, and for a second time,

William considered Matilda and Cyrus on the roof of the palace. Maybe he should go back to them. Maybe he didn't have the stones for this trip.

"Damn!" Artan said from inside the room.

William caught up to them and halted in the doorway. The walls of the small room were made from damp bricks. The ceiling made from the same grey stone they'd seen in many ruins like in the old city outside Edin. A bed took up one corner. A large basket rested against one wall, wooden toys spilling from the top of it like weeds from an overgrown plant pot. The paint had chipped away from many of them, and they were covered in dirt stains from years of use.

Where most of the walls were made from damp exposed brickwork, the wall near the basket of toys had a large sheet of black wood screwed onto it. A message had been written in chalk. Before William could get close enough to read it for himself, Olga read it aloud.

"Dear Grandfather Jacks, I'm writing this on here because you're dead and I wasn't the one to do it, so I have to get it out in some other way. How I would have loved to be the one to watch the life leave your eyes. To watch that sadistic and often lustful glow die with your final breath. To watch your old and wrinkled skin turn from pink to grey. To finally see the weak man in the husk of a human body as your last breath left your frail lungs. I remember this room from when I was a boy. You used to call it the playroom. Although there were toys in here, I think it was much more your playroom than it was ours. You'd keep your special boys in here, of which I was one. Sometimes I'd be waiting in this room for days. The door would open at mealtimes, the snap of the bolt striking fear into me in case it was you rather than one of your guards. Often it would be my next meal, but you would always turn up eventually. I hope you believe your lies about the high father, because if you do, your world must have a hell of some sort. And if it does, that's where you are now, paying the price tenfold for all the trauma and sadness you've spread. I'm leaving this room with my head held high. You're leaving this life stained with the shame of being a bully and a rapist. For once, I'm going to choose to believe in your prophet, and I pray to the high father that you feel every ounce of trauma you've inflicted on others." As she got to the end of the note, Olga's voice trembled and her words grew weak. "You called me by a different name, which is now long buried. This is my name. The name of a warrior. The name of a man far greater than anything you ever achieved in your life. I hope you feel even a fraction of the pain you've caused." Although she didn't read the last word, the message had clearly been signed by Hawk.

Closer to Olga than William, Artan rubbed her back. "Come on, let's go. There's nothing left in this room."

Barp!

Olga filled her lungs and nodded several times as if trying to push her tears down. When she finally turned from the blackboard, William led the way from the room. He had a place in this group. He had some value. He'd made the choice to go to the asylum, so they didn't need to question him again.

A small wooden door at the end of the corridor, William half expected it to be locked, but when he shoved it, it swung open. It led them into another gloomy hallway.

Barp!

The tone louder than before, they must have reached the asylum's basement. The screams of inmates and the cries of tortured children came from somewhere deep within the building. Distant as if they were echoes; memories of the madness spreading through this place like the plague beyond its walls.

Cells on their left and right, William got halfway down

the corridor before he checked back on the others. Olga had halted and Artan stood at her side. He returned to his friends. "Are you okay?"

Wide eyed, a slight glaze to her stare, Olga said, "They brought Matilda and me down here when they were holding us."

The floor of the cell glistened with damp. William's heart quickened to look into the place. What had they done to the girls in there? "Did anyone touch you?"

Olga shook her head. "They were too busy trying to break us. To make us compliant for Grandfather Jacks. They flooded the place and we nearly drowned. We had no control over what they did to us."

"Come on." William tugged on her arm. "We need to keep moving. Let's find Max, Hawk, and Dianna, and get the hell away from this place."

Barp!

At first, Olga resisted, but then she let William guide her. A sharp turn on their left, the hallway led up away from them. A route to the ground floor. So steep it burned William's tired calves, but a way out. A step closer to getting their friends and getting the hell out of there.

A dogleg bend in the tunnel blocked William's line of sight to the ground floor. The screams and shouts of the inmates had grown louder. They'd sounded farther away when they'd first entered the place. Footsteps thundered along the nearby corridors. William halted and let the other two catch up to him. "Can you hear that?"

"Come on." Olga shoved her way past. "Let's just keep moving."

Maybe they shouldn't be trying to deal with what they couldn't see, but surely if they could hear something, they should take that as a cue?

Olga rounded the bend first. William caught up to her. She'd halted closer to the top.

"Shit!" William said.

Maybe not every cell had been opened in the place, but from the number of inmates tearing through the hallways, a good proportion of them had.

"So what do we do now?" Artan said. The weak bulbs from the hallway caught the sheen of sweat on his face.

"What we'd planned to do all along." Olga set off. "Nothing's changed. We still need to find Max, Hawk, and Dianna."

CHAPTER 32

Max couldn't tell where his ragged breathing ended and Gracie's started, the echoes of both of them in the shadows at the back of the cell melding into one. Much louder and Monica would hear them, even with the insanity running through the halls.

Pressed close to one another, women and children streaming past the open cell door, they waited. About the only agency they had in that moment. The *click* of freeing locks worked their way down towards them. Each one, coupled with the *barp* of the deep tone, served as yet another countdown. Soon Monica would be on them. The gods would decide if she found them or not.

"Why don't we join the crowds?" Max said. "I could pretend to be an escaped prisoner. It's chaos out there."

Gracie shook her head. "You'll stand out from a mile away."

"I'm worried we've made the wrong choice waiting here."

"It's a bit late for that now. It's the decision we've made. We need to stick with it."

Barp!

Crack!

No matter how Max tried to master his breathing, his lungs tightened. He pulled at his shirt's collar, the fabric coming away from the tacky wound on his chest.

Crack!

They were getting closer. Stars swam in Max's vision, so he leaned against the wall for support. They'd made the wrong decision. They should have run while they could. Now they were trapped. But with Monica and her crew so close, they had no choice but to wait.

The screams of the formerly incarcerated women around them grew louder. The panic of children mingled with it, swirling through the riotous corridors. Maybe Gracie had a point. What would happen if this mob thought a guard walked among them? A guard who knew the way out.

"It'll be okay," Gracie said. "They can't see us, and it doesn't sound like they're going into any of the cells. They'll just assume this one is empty like all the others."

Crack!

Monica called, "The first person to bring me the boy will be rewarded."

Max whimpered.

Barp.

Dizzy with his lack of oxygen, Max shook his head repeatedly. *Mad Max.* They should have run. *Mad Max.* He gasped and held his chest. *Mad Max.*

And then calm. Everything slowed. The same *click* closed down on them from along the corridor. The same screams and cries. The same tone letting out a loud *barp.* Max reached across to take Gracie's knife.

"What are you doing?"

"I've already killed, have you?"

"Of course not."

"There seems little point in you having blood on your hands. If they come in here, I'll deal with them."

A proud young woman who could fight her own battles, yet Gracie eased the grip on her knife's handle and allowed him to take it.

His pulse beating slower, Max nodded to himself. Whatever happened, he had this.

The lights in the corridor outside lit up the ratty Monica as she passed the front of their cell. It spiked Max's pulse, but he held onto his panic with deep breaths. He had this. They'd be fine.

Crack!

Monica freed the woman who'd helped Max and the rest of her cellmates. Six of them flooded from the cell; desperate to be free, they ran after all the other inmates. Although they moved with intent, how could any of them know where they were going? Especially with the exit in the other direction.

But not all of the inmates had moved on. No more than five and a half feet tall, her black hair hung in matted chunks, so greasy it stuck to her face. Sores dotted her skin along her arms and on her cheek. Many of her teeth missing, her top lip rose in a snarl and her mouth fell open. She worked her jaw, hissing and growling.

"What the hell is she doing?" Gracie said.

"I dunno."

"I told you not to open the door!" the woman said, her right shoulder raised several inches higher than the left.

Where Monica had moved on, she now came back into view. Standing beside the woman, she looked from her, into the cell, and back to her again. A confused scowl, Monica clearly hadn't seen them yet. Tightening his grip on the knife, Max nodded. He'd be ready for her. She'd regret stepping into this cell.

The woman with the matted black hair shook. She

screamed so loud, not even the deep tone drowned her out. "I said it, didn't I? I said you shouldn't open the door. You shouldn't open it."

Max shook his head. As much as he'd fight Monica should he need to, he'd rather not. He whispered, "I didn't." He tightened his grip on the knife. "I didn't. Now please move on. Go."

The woman screamed and ran straight for them.

Max kicked off from the back wall to propel himself forwards.

The woman had a shorter distance to travel. She reached the cell door and slammed it shut, Max reaching out a moment too late.

Crack! The bolt locked on the other side.

The press of people closing in on the cell dulled the glow of the bulbs in the corridor. The screams close by had mostly died down, the chaos easing.

The woman with the greasy hair and the sores cried freely. "I-I-I …" She stuttered like she had hypothermia. "I-I told you. I t-told you on more th-than one o-o-o-occasion." Suddenly her words quickened and ran away from her, each one blurring into the next. "I said don't open the door and you opened it. You opened it. Why would you do that?"

"I didn't!" Max kicked the locked door, a loud *bang* shaking the thick wooden barrier in its frame. "Monica did."

One wide eye, the other one hidden behind her lank black hair, the woman peered into the cell, her ragged breaths carrying an underlying snort. "And now look where it's gotten you. You should have left it locked."

"Yeargh!" Max lunged forward with his knife hand, shoving it through the bars at the woman. But the woman ducked and a sharp sting ran through Max's wrist, delivered by a chopping hand.

The blow forced his grip loose and he dropped the knife. He withdrew his hand before they could attack him again.

The madwoman's face gave way to the only slightly more sane Monica. Her pointed nose and large yellow teeth. She grinned, her words interspersed with giggles. "Looks like you just gave up what little advantage you had, Max. Now that wasn't very smart, was it?"

His legs weak, Max stumbled away from the cell door. Several wobbly steps, the back of his knees caught the wooden bunk, and he fell into a sitting position, a deep sting buzzing through the burns on the insides of his thighs. He leaned the back of his head against the damp wall. Gracie looked at him, but he refused to look back. Coming into this cell had well and truly screwed them over. And now they were both going to pay the price. His eyes closed as he tried to shut out everything else; Max couldn't shut out the cackling titter of Monica. She'd won and she damn well knew it.

CHAPTER 33

"You say nothing's changed," William said as he ran after Olga, shouting to be heard over the chaos of the freed inmates and the loud *barp*, "and sure, we do need to still get Max, Hawk, and Dianna, but the state of this place is very different to what we were expecting. Surely we should at least take a moment to think this through?"

If Olga heard him, she didn't show it, charging up the ramp leading to the ground floor before she joined the chaos tearing through the old building. She turned left and vanished from sight. Were it not for the *crack* of a lock being freed, they would have lost her immediately. She'd unlocked the first cell she came to, three women charging out as she ran in and shouted, "Max!"

William blocked her from leaving the cell, Artan at his side. She raised her sword, the tip hovering in front of his face. "Come on, Olga. Think for a minute."

Olga's jaw jutted out and she raised her top lip in a snarl. The tip of her sword remained close to his throat, but she'd lowered it a little. "I will go through you both."

She wouldn't, and they both knew it. William stepped

forward and she moved back a pace. "What's gotten into you?" he said. "We all want the same thing here, but you need to hear us out."

"Something isn't right." She shook her head. "Max has been in here too long. I've been worried about him. From the state of this place, I'd say I have good reason to be concerned."

The shrill cry of a screaming woman ran past.

Artan lifted Olga's free hand in both of his. "Like William said, we all want the same thing. Now I might be wrong, but it doesn't seem like there are many men in this place."

The crowds contained women and children.

"I get that you think the crowd will hide us," Artan continued, "but they won't. They'll hide *you*. We need to at least wear a disguise of some sort if we're to move through here."

"Who are you hiding from?"

"I don't know," Artan said. "But I don't want to stand out to these people. Surely it pays to be cautious. You said yourself you think something's wrong. There has to be a reason why Max has been in here as long as he has."

Her chest rising and falling, Olga's upper body slowly unwound and she lowered her sword. "I'm sorry." A glance at William, she offered him the same. "Sorry."

"We're all keen to get Max and the others out, but I'm speaking from experience when I say we need to be cautious. My haste to get to you and Matilda nearly got Cyrus killed."

A yelling woman entered the room. Her hair like a bird's nest, her eyes wide, her skin streaked with dirt. William stepped back into a dark corner and dragged Artan with him. Leaning against the cold stone wall, they waited.

But instead of leaving the cell again, the woman stepped closer, her movements erratic. She screamed again, her panic animalistic.

When the woman opened her mouth for a third time, Olga lunged forwards and punched her square on the chin. The echo of the contact snapped William's shoulders tight, but it did the job. The woman's legs turned bandy and she crumpled. The inmates in the corridor were none the wiser.

"That's one way of doing it," William said, stepping forwards with Artan to drag the woman into the shadows.

William and Artan walked away from the downed woman, keeping their heads low as they stepped into the corridor. The rip of tearing fabric called to them from the cell.

Olga pulled William and Artan back and handed them both a strip of the woman's top. It left the woman naked from the waist up, her sagging breasts exposed on her skinny form.

"What's this for?" Artan said, raising his hand so he didn't have to look at the unconscious woman.

Olga snapped a sharp shrug, her words clipped with her impatience. "Make a headscarf out of it."

Had William had a better suggestion, he might have offered it. And when Artan said nothing either, he shrugged and pulled the woman's dirty top over his head, tying it around his chin. "You don't think our frames and broad shoulders give us away?"

Olga snorted a laugh. "I think your perception of how you look doesn't match up with the reality." She shook her head. "With what's going on in this place, I don't think you need the best disguise to be invisible."

"Mama?" A boy looked into the room. Seven or eight years old, he peered at William, Artan, and Olga as if trying to ascertain if any of them were his mum. Maybe the disguises worked and maybe they didn't; either way, the boy pulled back into the corridor and ran with the rest of the crowd, his call disappearing into the madness. "Mama. Mama."

"See," Olga said.

"You think that's evidence we're invisible?" William said.

"It passed the test."

"At least we didn't have to knock him out too," Artan said. "I think Olga's right. It's dark enough and crazy enough for us to be invisible with these scarves on. Let's find Max and the others and get out of here."

CHAPTER 34

Barp! The tone continued to call through the corridors, cutting through even the shrill chaos of the directionless prisoners. Although now William had gotten amongst it, he saw madness in far fewer people than he'd expected. The minority were the most vocal. Many of the inmates were frightened and desperate. They were clearly driven by a justified need to get out of there. "Do you think any of them have found a way out yet?" he said.

Artan said, "It doesn't look like it."

The boys tried to keep up with Olga. Smaller and faster than them, she moved through the pack like a rat. She charged into another cell and came back out before the boys reached her. She set off along the packed corridor again.

Crack! Olga unlocked the next cell, releasing another stream of prisoners.

"Olga!" William grabbed her shoulder. "Can you please slow down?"

"Would you slow down if this was Matilda?" Tears stood in her eyes. "Look at this place, William. Wherever Max is, we need to get to him and help him."

Crack!

One of the women from the next cell charged Olga, punching her as she came out. It knocked Olga down, William and Artan shielding her to prevent her getting trampled.

Olga jumped back to her feet, and William caught her around the waist before she could chase after the woman who'd knocked her down. She shook and twisted in his grip, but soon relaxed when he said, "The woman's already gone. She probably just got spooked. Remember, we're here to look for Max."

Olga threw her arms in the air, her sword desperately close to blinding a passer-by. "How the hell are we supposed to find him in a place like this?"

"Not by fighting the inmates. Don't you think they've had a hard enough time already?" William took Olga's hand and led her on, rounding the next bend.

Where every cell had a single door, one up ahead had two. They were wide open, the bright light inside the room spilling out into the corridor. Olga took off towards it.

William and Artan fought to get through the crowd, weaving through the bodies and catching up to Olga, who'd halted outside the cell. Her arms hung limp at her sides. As large as the gym in the national service area, the room must have been a dining room, or recreation area for the inmates. Max sat in a chair in the centre.

William reached out to catch Olga's shoulder, but gripped air as she burst into the room. He charged after her, Artan behind.

Six feet into the large space and the double doors slammed shut behind them.

A small ratty woman stepped away from the back wall, a knife to the throat of a young ginger woman who had her hair tied in a thick plait. The ratty woman had a shrill laugh that carried over the loud tone. "You really thought you could run around this place without me finding out?" Fifteen to twenty women were lined along the back wall. They stepped forward with the woman holding the knife. "You have two young men with you. They stand out like a sore thumb in a place like this."

Olga turned to Max while pointing at the ginger captive. "Who the fuck is that?"

"She's a friend, Olga. She's been trying to help me get out of here."

Olga shook her head, her voice growing louder, her fury bubbling over. "She might be your friend, but she's definitely not mine."

"Please, Olga." Max pressed his hands together as if in prayer. "She's put her neck on the line to try to help me."

"She clearly didn't do a very good job. I would have done better."

The ratty woman shouted to be heard. "Whatever's going on with you two needs to stop now. You need to drop your weapons and put your hands behind your backs before I cut Gracie's throat."

"I don't give a shit what you do to Gracie," Olga said.

The woman drew a deep breath in through her large nose. "Take a look around, sweetie. You're outnumbered. There's only one winner here, whether Gracie lives or not. Maybe you should care about that? I'm just trying to make you feel a bit better by pretending you have a choice."

William took the lead, Jezebel hitting the stone floor with a *clang*.

The clatter of Artan's knives followed.

One of the women who'd hidden against the wall came forwards and took the weapons away. For a second, William thought Olga might lunge at her, but she held her ground.

"Fuck it," she finally said, throwing Matilda's sword down and holding her hands out in front of her.

Three women with ropes came forwards and bound their wrists.

CHAPTER 35

William stood alongside Max, Olga, Artan, and Gracie. They'd been lined up along the far wall in the brightly lit room, their wrists tied behind their backs. So tired from the day, William leaned his head against the cold stones.

The ratty woman, Monica, paced up and down in front of them. She took small and sharp steps, her heels clicking against the stone floor. Her hair shook with her stamping feet. "So"—she massaged her temples as if warding off a headache—"let me get this straight. You've swanned in here" —her voice grew louder, her rage running away with her— "rubbing it in our faces about how easy it's been for you to enter the asylum, and you bring young *men* with you. Some of the inmates in this place might have been driven insane by Grandfather Jacks' cruelty, but we're not all mad. You think we can't tell the difference between men and women?"

They'd locked the double doors. It did little to shut out the *barp,* but at least it muted the chaos in the hallways.

Her eyes wide, her yellow-toothed overbite clamped down on her bottom lip, Monica's voice wavered. "Know you're all on very thin ice. I'm about out of patience." Her nostrils flared and she now levelled the knife she'd previously held to Gracie's throat on Max. "You came here for Max, and you've already shown me how little Gracie means to you. That information will be valuable for when I'm choosing who to hurt."

They'd lined Olga and Gracie up side by side. From where William stood, he'd not yet seen either girl look at the other.

"So here's what I'm going to do. Seeing as none of you will tell me how you got here, I'm going to try the front door one final time. But this is your last chance. Once I leave here, the talking's over. If you don't give me answers now, I will be back to rain down hell on you. And I'll start with Max here."

They could tell her about the tunnel. With Matilda and Cyrus on the roof of the palace, they wouldn't be that easy to find. But what then? What happened to them when they gave up their only valuable piece of information?

Olga answered William's question for him. "Like Max said, if we tell you how to get out of here, what use are we to you then? Why would you keep us alive?"

"There's more than one of you."

Olga shook her head and spat on the floor at Monica's feet. "You will never divide us."

"You say that now." A nasty twist took over Monica's face. "I've been through or witnessed every torture technique Grandfather Jacks has used in the years I've been here. I've seen more women broken than you've seen sunrises. You think I don't know how to get the information I need?" She shrugged. "Maybe you're right, but that won't stop me from trying. This is your last chance. How do we get out of here?"

As they'd done the last fifteen times she'd asked, Max's bloody nose evidence of how they held out on Monica, the group remained silent.

"Fine," Monica said, turning her back on them. "Don't say I didn't warn you."

Monica left the room, leaving just three armed guards behind. William should have done what Cyrus had done when they were in the wild meadow and the nomads tied them up. It might have broken a finger to jam it into the rope's knot, but he could have stopped them tying his bonds completely if he'd thought about it. What an idiot.

"He's all right," Olga said.

William leaned away from the wall to get a better look at Max and Olga. What the hell were they talking about?

"You would say that." Max sniffed some of the blood back into his nose.

"What's that supposed to mean?"

"Don't you remember kissing him?"

"Look, you two," Gracie said, "why don't—"

"Did I ask you for your fucking opinion?" Olga said. The whipcrack of her voice echoed in the large room. "I know you're trying to move in on my man—"

"I thought your man was Hawk!" Max's voice had grown louder too, amplified by the large space.

"Hey!" one of the three women on the door said, slamming the base of her spear against the stone floor with a *snap!* "Why don't you two shut up?"

"I only kissed Hawk because you were being a prick," Olga said. "If you learned how to communicate, none of this would have happened."

"So you're taking no responsibility for your lips touching his? It was a complete accident over which you had no control?"

"Don't be a dick, Max."

"And what am I supposed to do anyway?"

"Hey!" the guard said again.

"It's not like we could have had a normal relationship."

"You're saying I'm not normal?" Olga said.

In that moment, everything changed and William finally saw this for what it was. Three armed guards against five bound prisoners should have been manageable, but the guard with the spear had broken away from the other two, who remained by the double doors. Five against one.

"You two are really pissing me off," the woman said. "You're about to be tortured by Monica and you're choosing now as the time to have a lovers' tiff?" The woman turned her spear around, aiming the flint tip at the arguing pair. "Monica doesn't care if you're not all here when she gets back. As long as there are enough of you to question."

From Artan's relaxed posture, he clearly understood this argument too.

Gracie, on the other hand, did not. Shaking her head, she backed into the wall as if pushing hard enough would get her out of there. Would somehow distance her from the others' antics. "Please, you two. I was trying to help Max. There's no need to argue about it." The woman with the spear drew closer. "Don't let me die here. I want to come with you guys. I want to—"

William yelled and charged the guard.

Artan did the same, the pair of them closing down on her.

The guard turned one way and then the other. She had to go for one of them, but which?

Maybe because he made the most noise, the guard lurched at William, who ducked her attack, sliding into her shins with a two-footed tackle. The woman fell on him, sandwiching him between her and the hard ground.

Artan kicked her in the head, knocking her out cold.

As she lay on the stone floor, the chaos still outside the room, the *barp* calling through the large building, William got to his feet and turned around, showing Artan his bound hands. "Here, untie me."

But Artan's features fell slack when the double doors opened. A group of about ten more women to add to the two guards already inside the room. They must have been waiting in the corridor.

"You'd do well to calm down," one of the women said. All of them were armed. They spread out across the room and stepped forwards as one. "There's no way you can win this. If you recognise that now, we might let you live."

"Shit!" Olga hissed.

Artan stepped away, returning to his spot on the wall.

William followed suit, backing into the cold stone. He said, "That was our last chance. I wonder if we need to start giving Monica what she wants."

The doors to the large room remained open. Many people ran past, screaming and shouting. Many of them had lost their mind. He'd arguably lost his mind more than most, but when Hawk stepped into the room, Cyrus' sword in his grip, William's shoulders relaxed. The guards were too focused on William and the others to have seen him. Where he'd been topless, he now wore a shirt. His face glistened with sweat.

William spoke beneath his breath. "Maybe we will get out of here after all."

CHAPTER 36

"Hawk," William said, "behind you!" But even as he said it, his words faded.

Monica levelled her knife on the back of Hawk's neck and growled, "Drop your weapon."

Hawk spun away from her and raised his sword in return. "You drop yours."

William gulped, his throat dry. The insanity remained in the hallways outside. It could spill into their room at any moment.

A shrill cackle, Monica shook her head. "Have you seen how outnumbered you are?"

"I'll still be able to cut your throat."

William and the others remained pressed against the wall. Monica hadn't noticed her downed guard yet. Maybe this would be their last chance to fight their way out.

Monica spoke with a soft tone. "You and I are similar."

"How do you work that out?"

Using the tip of her knife to highlight his scars, Monica said, "We've both suffered at the hands of Grandfather Jacks."

"What do you know of my suffering?"

"I have similar scars on the inside. We shouldn't be fighting against one another; we should be uniting and taking down that madman. We should be working against his agents." She waved her blade in the direction of William and his friends.

The slightest lowering of his sword, Hawk's head dropped. "You're right. I just want to see an end to that madman."

The same confused frown on the faces of all his friends. Gracie seemed none the wiser.

"I knew you were a fucking snake," Max said. "I knew you couldn't be trusted. You're only out for yourself."

"And I know what those scars are about," Monica said.

A flicker ran through Hawk's seemingly calm features. He coughed to clear his throat.

Monica shook her head and dropped her gaze before returning it to Hawk. "I've seen too many little boys go off to be one of Grandfather Jacks' angels. Too many boys separated from their mothers."

Tears filled Hawk's eyes.

"Do you know what he does to the mums?"

Hawk shook his head. "Stop. Please."

"Grandfather Jacks is dead," Max said.

"He's tortured all of us." Monica's eyes also filled. Her lips bent out of shape. "We have a lot in common."

"Please stop." Hawk shook his head repeatedly. "I can't hear it. Please stop. The others are right, Grandfather Jacks is dead."

Although Monica's tears had broken and ran down her cheeks, she laughed. "Don't be so gullible. You shouldn't believe a word that comes from their mouths. They know nothing. They're liars. He's not dead. He's alive and well, and when we get out of here, we're going to make him pay for all the things he's done. We're going to take our time and make sure he experiences pain equal to that which he's spread."

Hawk banged the heel of his right palm against his forehead. "Shut up!" He scratched at the scars around his neck. "Just stop talking."

"The only way it'll stop is if we end him. If we get out of here. We need them to tell us where the keys are to get out of this place, and then you can make him pay. Remember everything he did to you. Relive it, use it as fuel to find a way out of here."

The bright light glistened off the blood on Hawk's scars.

Monica goaded him, "That's right. Remember what he's done. Use it."

Hawk yelled and charged. One of Monica's guards brought the handle of her weapon around and slammed it into Hawk's face with a loud *tonk!*

"Oomph." The air left Hawk's lungs when he landed on his back.

The guard who'd knocked him down turned Jezebel around and showed him the large axe blade. "Move and I'll split your head like a pumpkin."

CHAPTER 37

After capturing Hawk, Monica and her guards bound them all tighter than before. The ropes cutting into his wrists, his hands behind his back, William sat in a line with the others against the far wall of the large room. Max sat on his right at the end of the line, Gracie and all the others on his left. His bottom numb from the cold stone, his back either damp or cold, hard to tell which. Either way, if he leaned against the wall for too long, more pains spread through him, the large stones lumpy and unforgiving.

In an attempt to relieve the aches in his back, a particularly nagging pain biting into the space beneath his right shoulder blade, William leaned forward and arched his spine. Monica and the guards were at the other side of the room. One of the women held Jezebel; another one had Max's war hammer.

"I'm sorry," Hawk said. He waited for the loud *barp* to pass. "That woman got in my head. I couldn't think straight when she started talking about Grandfather Jacks and all he's done."

"You tried," Olga said.

Although where Olga supported Hawk, Max leaned away from the wall and stared down the line at the boy. He offered him the same disdain Olga had levelled on Gracie since the two of them had met.

"Do you want to say something to him?" Olga said.

Max shook his head and pulled back, muttering, "Like you have with Gracie, you mean?"

"What?" Olga said.

William spoke so only Max could hear him. "Surely you can see how traumatised Hawk is?"

Max's lips pursed and he shook his head once. He dragged in a sharp sniff and lifted his chin, staring across the large room at the double doors on the other side. "I don't care."

"Look, Max," William said, "you need to trust me on this one when I say drop it. The depths Hawk has gone to to try to help us stretches beyond anything I've ever known. Whatever's going on with you and Olga, you need to work it out between you and not involve him. His problems are far larger than that."

"Why are you on his side all of a sudden?"

"We've had a glimpse into what it meant to be a boy in this place. To be one of Grandfather Jacks' angels. For Hawk to help us get here, he had to revisit his past. Not only that, but he had to do it in front of me, Olga, and Artan. Were I in Hawk's position, I don't know if I would have been as brave as him, or as sane. He should be a wreck of a person."

"That's all well and good, but where has his bravery got us?"

"Don't judge him on the end result."

"What should I judge him on, then?"

"His intention. His loyalty. He could have just sold us out to Monica and joined sides with her. That would have probably led to him getting Dianna back. But he didn't do that, did he?"

"Then he's stupid."

"And remember, Olga kissed him, not the other way around."

"What's that got to do with it?"

"Come on, Max."

All the while the *barp* shook the walls of the place. The hallways remained alive with the insanity of the liberated prisoners. They clearly still hadn't worked out where they were running. How long would it take for one of them to find the tunnel to the palace? Any slight leverage they might have with Monica would be gone the second someone found a way through. And what would that mean for Matilda and Cyrus?

The sides of Max's jaw tightened and his nostrils flared. He breathed through his nose.

"Do you know where she is?" William said.

Max shrugged. "Who?"

"Dianna."

Max focused on Monica and her gang by the door. He shook his head. "No, but I have seen her. They used her as bait to lure me into a cell before they jumped me. It's how I ended up as Monica's prisoner." His eyes narrowed, but his scowl lifted. "You say we should understand where Hawk has come from, right?"

"Sure."

"If I know what he's about and empathise with that, I might find it easier to like him?"

"It's worked for me."

"Yo, Monica!"

William's heart raced and he shifted away from Max, putting some distance between them.

Monica turned slowly.

"What the hell are you doing?" William said.

The woman's shoulders pulled into her neck as she stepped towards her prisoners. Her cruelty fought for possession of her features, the tight wind in her frame spreading across her face.

"Max." Olga spoke this time. "What are you playing at?"

Max remained focused on Monica. "You've been in here a long time, right? Long enough for it to be detrimental."

"What do you reckon?" The *barp* snapped her rigid. After all this time she clearly hadn't gotten used to the sound. Maybe she no longer had any awareness of her reaction to it.

"Neither of us knows who to trust, but the truth is, we all want the same thing. We all want to get out of here, and we all hate Grandfather Jacks and what he did to the people in this place. How do we help you believe that?"

"Give me the key to get out of here."

"Okay."

"What are you doing, Max?" William said. "If you let her out of here, what leverage do we have?"

"Maybe it's time to treat her like a human being. To show her we're all on the same page. To show her a way out of here, extend the olive branch. Maybe we should let her see we understand what she's been through and we want to help."

Monica bounced on the spot, her features softening and crunching, changing from second to second, unable to settle on one emotional state. "And what if you're tricking me?"

"You can kill me. You can kill us all."

"I was planning on doing that anyway."

"Then you have nothing to lose. And maybe when I help you get out of here, you'll see we're not your enemy and you might change your mind about us?"

"Get up," Monica said.

Max rocked forwards and stood up. William pulled

against his restraints to drag his friend back down again, but the ropes around his wrists were too tight.

"Are you sure you know what you're doing?" William said.

Max shook his head. "No, but what have we got to lose? Maybe instead of fighting her, I need to try understanding her. Like you've had a glimpse of what Hawk's been through, I've had a glimpse of Monica's suffering. It ain't pretty."

The wall cold and hard against his back, William let out a long exhalation and rested his head against the damp stones. They had very little to lose now. They were going to die at Monica's hand either way. Maybe Max could get them out of there. Where they had none, at least now they could hold some hope in their hearts, no matter how small.

CHAPTER 38

His hands still tied behind his back, Max left the large room through the double doors, Monica beside him. She'd brought six of her guards with them. Three in front and three behind, the shadows hid the women's faces like they had for most of the time they'd been in there. Maybe they felt the shame at what they were a part of. Maybe most of them were more like Gracie than Sally. Or maybe it was simply the poor light hiding their features. Whatever it was, they were close enough to react should Monica call on them.

The three women at the front helped clear a path through the busy main corridor, allowing Max and Monica to walk with ease. "Why have you only freed some of the women and children in this place?" Max said.

Monica's back snapped with a tight twist at the next loud *barp!* The tension remained with her, her words sharp. "You're going to tell me how to run this place now?"

"The point I'm making," Max said, "is that you know what it's like to be in here. You know what it is to suffer in a dark cell. Why would you put other innocent women and children through the same torture?"

"You know I will kill you if you try to screw me over, don't you?"

They were already close to the exit, the door leading to the outside larger and thicker than the others. Max said, "You need to show me where Dianna is."

She might have been much smaller than him, but Monica's speed and strength caught Max off guard. She grabbed his shirt, turned him around, and slammed him, back first, into the steel door with a *boom*. Her right hand still gripping his shirt and pressing against the burn on his pec, she angled her knife up at his eye with her other hand. "I'll drive the tip of this straight into your brain." She spat when she spoke.

"I know where the key is."

Monica pressed the air from Max's lungs, leaning against his chest, digging her hand deeper into his burn. Her face red, her large yellow teeth gnashing at the air in front of her. "Then show me!"

"I will, I promise." He took several breaths to ride out the sting of his burn. "But I need to know Dianna's okay. She's the reason I came here."

"You sweet on her or something?"

"No. She's a friend. If we don't help friends in this world, then what do we have?" His voice broke when he said, "I have no family left."

His slight wobble disarmed Monica and she lowered her knife by an inch or two.

Barp!

The tone snapped her rigid again. She pressed the tip of her blade into his right cheek. It stung from where it broke his skin, burning as she pressed harder. More spittle than before, she sprayed his face when she said, "You talk about not depriving the women in here. About keeping them away from seeing daylight, but that's what you're doing to me now. You know how desperate I am to get out, and you're holding that over me." She pressed into his cheek even harder, a warm line of blood running down the side of his mouth. "How fucking dare you? Now show me how to get the hell out of here before I blind you." She lifted the tip of her knife again so Max could see it close up.

Adrenaline surged through Max and he shivered. His words trembled with his form, but he remained consistent. "The same is true now as it's always been. The second I open this door—" he kicked the large barrier behind him "—you no longer need me or any of my friends."

Her dark ratty eyes shifting from one of Max's to the other, she shook her head and stepped away. "I'm done with this. We'll knock a wall down and take our chances with the diseased. Just kill him."

The guards had already formed a semicircle around Max and Monica. As Monica stepped away, they closed in.

CHAPTER 39

William rocked where he sat, twinges of pain firing off at random points along his body. They'd been here for what felt like hours already. The floor still cold and hard and his bottom numb. The wall behind him uneven from where no two stones in the wall lay flush with one another. The second he leaned back, a lump jabbed into his spine and he groaned. "Urgh!"

Olga sat at the other end of the line to William. She had Artan next to her, then Hawk, then Gracie. "At what point do we accept he might not come back?"

Ten to fifteen guards at the other end of the room by the double doors. If Olga cared about being heard by them, she hid it well. All of them looked over when she spoke. The one Monica had left in charge, a short woman in her thirties, walked over, her boot heels clicking against the stone floor. "Shut up!"

Barp!

Olga rocked forwards to get to her feet. Artan knocked her back down again. Thankfully he sat next to her. If anyone could keep her in check ...

Her face puce, her lips tight, Olga glared at Matilda's brother, who stared straight back, his features relaxed. He'd do it again if she tried to stand. She turned her fury on the guard. "Fuck you! Tell me to shut up again and—"

"What?" A knife in each hand, the guard threw her arms out in a shrug. "You'll what?"

"I've had enough of this bullshit," Olga said. "If it wasn't for your insane boss, we wouldn't be in this situation. We're on the same side. Why can't you see that?"

Although the guard stepped closer to Olga, she threw a glance at Gracie. The ginger-haired girl shook her head.

"Why are you looking at her?" Olga said. "You want to have this out, have it out with me! You don't need her approval."

The guard looked at Gracie again and raised her eyebrows. Again Gracie shook her head, the guard returning to be with the others by the double doors.

Barp!

Although Olga leaned out and looked down the line at Gracie as if she might start something, William spoke before she could. "I think we need to accept that Max has bought us time. I'm not sure he's brought us much else. How we get out of here from now is down to us. And if we find a way, we might need to get to him and save his arse."

"In case you haven't noticed—" Olga got to her feet, several of the guards watching her as she showed William her bound wrists "—our hands are tied. We won't get very far like this."

"We wait here and we're screwed," Artan said.

"Helpful!" Olga said. "You got anything we can act upon?"

"I can't take this anymore," Gracie said.

Olga shook her head. "And you think we can?"

Gracie rocked where she sat. It took her several attempts before she rocked forwards, stood in a crouch, and fell back against the wall. Higher than before, she flipped her body away to a standing position.

"Fat lot of good standing up is going to do." Olga's jaw fell as Gracie walked over to the guards. "Where the hell is she going?"

Still on her feet, Olga stepped after Gracie, but William said, "Leave it," while Artan blocked her with his legs.

"I don't trust her," Olga said.

"That's because you're jealous of her. You didn't like finding her here with Max."

"Fuck you, William."

"Look, just stay here. Let's see what she's intending to do before we overreact, yeah?"

Before Olga could reply, Gracie spoke to the guards, loud enough for them all to hear. "Remember, I'm one of you."

"See," Olga said.

"I was captured and kept in here like every one of you were," Gracie continued. "I didn't turn on you, I turned on Monica. Surely you understand why I did that."

"That's because she's a fucking snake," Olga said, shouting over to the guards. "Look at her. She'll change allegiance in a heartbeat. Don't trust her."

"I thought you just told that guard we were on the same side?" Artan said.

If Hawk had opinions on the matter, he kept them to himself. He'd remained statue still while events unfolded, staring into space through glazed eyes.

"That was before they refused to free me," Olga said.

When Gracie turned around and the guard cut her bonds, William's heart sank. It had grown increasingly difficult to defend her, especially when the guard handed her a sword.

"You were saying, William?" Olga said. "She's one of them, and now we're fucked!"

CHAPTER 40

A semicircle of swords pointing his way kept Max's back against the asylum's cold steel main door. "I know you want to kill me," he said, "but you also want to get out of here, so think carefully about this."

"We'll find another way," Monica said.

"You might. But what if that other way lets in all the diseased around this place? I've been out there recently. I've seen how bad it is."

Barp!

Monica spat when she spoke. "It's better than giving in to you."

"It might be, but all I'm asking is for you to let Dianna out."

"I've already said I will."

"You'll forgive me for not trusting you. Considering what you've already put me through."

Monica bit down on her bottom lip with her large yellow teeth. Her dark eyes remained fixed on Max when she waved the guards back. Many of them appeared relieved to receive the order. "I'll take you to Dianna, but I will kill you once you've let me out of this place. I can't have you challenging me so openly and getting away with it."

Of course Max didn't want to die, but the threat of death had been hanging over him since he got caught in the cell. At least this deal took him a step closer to liberating Dianna. "As long as you let Dianna and the others go. That way, Dianna gets back to Hawk and you can punish me how you see fit." As he said it, twinges ran through the burn in his pec, and the insides of his thighs throbbed.

Monica pointed a long and bony finger at him. Her twisted yellow nail resembled a talon. "This is your last chance. If you're not good to your word, I'll kill all of you. I promise you that."

Max nodded, following Monica as she turned and led him down a dark corridor. Many of the doors were already open. Monica had let the inmates out, and they in turn had let out the others.

They took several deviations as they walked the packed corridors. Left, right, left, left, right, left. Although Max tried to remember the way, he'd lost track after the first few turns. The place might have been lit, but not well enough to allow him to discern one hallway from the next. "What are you hoping to achieve in how you're running this place?"

"Huh!"

"Being so controlling of everyone in here. What are you hoping to gain from it?"

The fury in Monica's features died. "Grandfather Jacks has had control over my life for a long, long time."

"And I'm sorry for that."

Monica's eyes narrowed as she studied his face as if searching for the lies in his words. The crow's feet at her temples softened and she said, "Thank you. I won't ever allow someone to have that control over my life again."

"And the only way to do that is to exert control over others like Grandfather Jacks did with you?"

Where there had been a flicker of humanity in her features, Monica's face tightened again. "It's dog eat dog. If I don't get on top, someone else will."

And how could he blame her for thinking like that? With the amount of time she'd spent incarcerated, why wouldn't she be petrified of it happening again?

Another left turn revealed the only locked cell on their journey. A guard stood on either side of the door. The hallway was still alive with activity, women and kids running as if the faster they moved, the more likely they'd be to find the building's exit. Monica nodded at the guards, who opened the cell door with a *crack!*

Max waited outside. Best not put himself in a room they could lock behind him. At the back of the cell stood at least ten women. All of them had their hands bound like Max and his friends.

Monica remained at Max's side. "Get Dianna."

"What have all these women done?" Max said.

"They refused to join the cause."

"What are you going to do with them?"

"I'm undecided."

Maybe too dark to be certain, but one of the guards on the cell door winced. Other than Sally, there hadn't been many guards who seemed as into Monica's plans as the crazy woman. They did what was necessary to ensure their own survival, but they clearly weren't buying into Monica's regime. If Max let things drag on long enough, would he witness the others overthrowing their insane leader? Hopefully the revolution would come before he lost his life.

The same *barp*, the same screams from the inmates, Max and Dianna walked side by side as they were led away from the cell, which Monica had locked again. The guards surrounded them, giving them a clear path through the busy hallways.

"I'm sorry they used me as bait," Dianna said quietly enough so only Max heard.

"Don't be." Max shook his head. "I've seen who's running the show here. You know, Hawk is with the others."

"He is!"

Dianna's raised tone caused Monica to turn around. Her top lip lifted, her large nose aimed straight at them like an accusatory finger.

"He's the reason we came in here to get you. He said you were good to him in Umbriel."

"He's not as bad as you think, you know."

Monica and her guards stopped outside the double doors leading to the large room with all their friends in. She kicked them open with a *thud!* Both doors flew inwards and slammed against the walls on the inside.

The guards rushed out. Many Max didn't recognise, they charged Monica, their weapons raised. And then he saw, "Gracie?" He saw the large battle axe first. "William?"

Hawk, Artan, and Olga were among the guards. While they pinned Monica to the wall, Olga came over to Max, dipped a nod at Dianna, and handed him his war hammer. She then kissed him on the cheek and wrapped him in a hug.

Max's face grew hot and he gritted his teeth against Olga leaning against the burn on his pec. "Thank you," he said. "What's happened?"

Gracie spoke to Monica. "We don't want to hurt you, but no one's into running this place your way. And because of that ..." Three guards led Monica at knife point over to a cell on the other side of the hallway and slammed the door shut, sliding the bolt across.

"It turns out we're all on the same side," Olga said, moving over so Dianna could run to Hawk, the pair hugging one another. "I was wrong about Gracie. She got the guards to listen to her."

But Max stepped away from Olga. "What are you doing?" she said.

"You have another way out of here, right? That doesn't involve going across the meadow?"

"We do. We're going to show the other guards too so they can slowly help the women and children get free."

"Good." Max headed to Monica's cell.

"What are you doing?" William said.

"I made a promise to her," Max said. "She gave Dianna back, and I've promised I'll show her sunlight. She's spent more of her life in the dark than she has out of it. She's not seen the outside since Grandfather Jacks imprisoned her."

"But what if she turns on you?" Artan said.

"She has no backup." Max shook his head. "She's not a threat anymore." He opened the door with a *crack* and held his hand into the cell. "I made you a promise. I'll take you out the front of this place." Then to the others, "I'll be okay. I'll meet you on the roof of the palace in a bit, yeah?"

Olga came forwards and held Max's hand. "You want me to come with you?"

"No." He shook his head. "I need to do this. I'll probably get to the palace's roof before you do."

A slight nod, Olga then kissed Max's cheek for a second time.

He smiled at her. "I could get used to this. Now go. I'll see you all soon." Armed with his war hammer and a knife he'd taken from one of the guards, Max said, "Come on, Monica. As long as you don't give me any shit, you're going to see daylight again."

CHAPTER 41

Only three guards had come down to the tunnel's entrance connecting the asylum to the palace. They had a lot to manage with the inmates, and they agreed they'd give William and the others a chance to get away before that process started. And good riddance. William, for one, had spent far more time in this place than he cared to. The sooner they moved on, the better. Hopefully Matilda's thigh had healed enough to make her mobile.

Gracie hugged one of the guards. They'd shared a cell together in the asylum. "Are you sure you don't want me to stay and help?"

"You've done enough already," the guard said. "Good luck, yeah?"

The two women hugged again before Hawk led them into the tunnel.

Although William took up the rear, Gracie and Dianna ahead of him, he still heard Olga and Artan's conversation. The tight and dingy tunnel amplified their words, and when the guards closed the door behind them, it muted the loud *barp!*

"I hope Max is going to be okay," Olga said.

"He's in control of Monica. She has no one on her side now, so I'm sure there's nothing to worry about."

"I hope you're right. I'll just be glad to get away from this place. I mean, the palace has potential for anyone who wants to stay, but they have to work out how to shut off that fucking noise while keeping the power on."

"And they have to deal with the damage done to so many people by Grandfather Jacks."

When Olga didn't reply, William stood on his tiptoes to see over the heads of the others. They were passing the room on their left with the toys in. The room in which Hawk had written his note to Grandfather Jacks.

Olga rested her hand on the broad-shouldered hunter's back. "Are you okay?"

He nodded and his tone remained even. "I think I will be."

The group pushed on, leaving the tunnel via the door at the other end. Olga, Artan, and Hawk all watched the room on their right as they passed it. When William walked past, he shuddered. What they'd had to do to those boys in there … But they weren't boys. Not by the time they found them. They did them a favour.

The pace too quick to dwell on it, Gracie and Dianna pulled up when they reached the diseased with the popped eyeballs at the bottom of the stairs.

A gentle shove in their backs to keep them moving, William said, "We did what was necessary."

Hawk—at the front of the line—lifted his head as if listening to their conversation. There seemed little point in talking about his wholly unnecessary attack on the diseased. It stood in their way and Hawk ended it. They didn't need to say any more.

William stepped out into the wide main corridor, overtook the others to reach the door to Grandfather Jacks' comfort room, and hit the button on the outside three times. He entered and positioned himself in front of the wardrobe. The four fallen diseased remained on the floor. They could deal with them, but no one else needed to see the impaled kid hanging on the coat peg.

The small side table wobbled when William—as the last one out of there—stood on it to climb out of the small window. Artan reached down for him, catching his hand and dragging him up onto the palace's roof. The bright light burned William's eyes, but he kept his face pointed at the sky anyway. A lump in his throat, the wind in his hair, he let out a long sigh, his voice cracking when he hugged Artan and said, "We did it!"

CHAPTER 42

"It's under there," Max said, using the tip of his knife to show Monica where to look.

The ratty woman reached under the bed in the cell, hooking her hand around until the key hit the stone floor with a *cling*.

Her entire body shook when she got to her feet, the key in her trembling grip. She walked to the asylum's exit and it took her several attempts to get the key into the lock. When she turned it, the large bolt came free with a *crack*! The hinges groaned as she shoved the door wide and stumbled out into daylight.

Tears streamed down Monica's face and she turned on the spot while staring up at the sky. Her voice weak, she croaked, "My god, I didn't think I'd ever see sunlight again."

Where Monica's eyes had appeared black in the asylum, the sunlight revealed them for the deep hazel they were. She then bolted, sprinting away from Max. She ran on wobbly legs towards the end of the steel tunnel. The *barp* calling across the landscape had summoned many of the diseased to the front of the asylum, but there were still several running alongside her, stumbling, their arms wild as they tried to keep pace with the ratty woman. Two of them tripped and fell, the others reaching the gate at the end in time for Monica to shake the door, the large steel frame rattling.

His war hammer in one hand, his knife in the other, Max slowly walked towards the end of the tunnel.

"Please," the ratty woman said, pressing her hands together in prayer and dropping to her knees in front of him, "please don't make me go back inside that place. I can't take it anymore. I can't take being a prisoner."

"What would you have me do, Monica?"

"You can open this gate?"

"I can."

"Then let me go."

The afternoon sun glistened off the tear tracks streaking Monica's cheeks. The diseased that had fallen had gotten back to their feet and waited at the end of the tunnel, snarling, hissing, banging their fists against the filigreed barrier between them.

"What about the diseased?"

"I'd take a three-minute run in the meadow over the rest of my life in prison. I'm not stupid, Max, I can see how broken I am. Those are the worst times. When I get a glimpse of sanity. When the clouds part and I'm who I used to be. It makes me see just how fucking crazy I am now." She slammed a closed fist against the side of her head. "I don't want it anymore. Allow me this choice. I'm no good to anyone. I've been deprived of free will for so long. Please allow me to decide my fate for once. Please?"

A lump had swelled in Max's throat. How different was he to Monica? What would it take for the madness he felt around the diseased to turn into his full-time outlook? And if he ever did get there, would someone do him the courtesy of allowing him to end it?

Returning to the place he'd buried the key, the six or seven diseased remaining at the end of the tunnel with Monica, Max pulled it from the ground.

After unlocking the gate, Max kept a hold of it and said, "You're sure you want this?"

"I am."

Before Max could pull the gate wide, Monica threw her scrawny arms around him. "Thank you. You're a good man. I don't deserve even a shred of kindness from you because of how I've been. Thank you."

The hinges on the steel gate groaned. To give Monica a head start, Max went out first and kicked away the diseased gathered around the end of the tunnel, driving them back.

Monica broke through the creatures and ran through the long grass of the meadow. The same cackling laugh Max had associated with her insanity, it now came out of her with the wild abandon of a child. She spread her arms wide as if hugging the sun. For the first time in years, she was finally free.

Clop! A diseased slammed into Monica from her right. It hit her so hard her hair flayed out in a wild arc. She crashed to the ground and twisted to be free of the first diseased, but quickly ended up beneath another one. And then another.

Max let out a hard sigh as he locked the gate behind him. He had both keys in his pocket, ready to leave them at the palace for the asylum's inmates.

His legs tired, his eyes sore, treacle ran through Max's veins as he slowly trudged towards his friends. The *barp* from the asylum on his left, scatterings of diseased close by. When he got to within six feet of one, *Mad Max* returned, the diseased wearing his brother's face.

Max slid the blade down his belt at the back of his trousers. He gripped his war hammer with both hands and brought it down on top of the closest diseased. His eyes burned with tears and his throat locked. He sobbed as he walked.

~

Maybe he would have seen it sooner were his eyes not blurred with his grief. Now he'd gotten closer to the palace, he couldn't avoid it. Cyrus stood on the roof, a shirtless hunter behind him with a knife to his throat. Max froze. "Fuck!"

CHAPTER 43

"It feels so good to be out of there," William said. He filled his lungs, his eyes still sore from the change in light.

Artan had helped William up and waited with him on the roof. The others had already set off back to where they'd left Matilda and Cyrus.

"William!" Olga's shrill panic sent ice through his veins.

William took off, Artan beside him. His feet twisted and turned on the angled roof. He charged over the first peak and halted. "Shit!" And then to the man who had a knife to Cyrus' neck, "Why are you doing this to him?"

The hunter, topless like Hawk had been for so long, shook when he shouted, "Come any closer and I'll slit his fucking throat."

Smaller than even Cyrus, but stocky like Hawk, the hunter stood much closer to Matilda than any of William and his group. She sat on the roof, holding her thigh.

"Hawk?" the hunter then said. "Dianna? What are you two doing here? What, you're some kind of turncoats, are you? Traitors?"

Hawk stepped a pace towards the hunter, who pulled his knife tighter to Cyrus' throat and said, "Stay back!"

Cyrus cried, his nose glistening with snot, his chin trembling with his grief.

"It's not about being a traitor," Hawk said. "Grandfather Jacks never had my loyalty. I came here to free Dianna, and these people helped me. They've shown me more care, love, and respect than Grandfather Jacks ever did. Besides, he's dead. What are you doing here? How did you survive?"

The hunter's voice still ran loud and then quiet, wavering with his fury. "There was a group of us who managed to find somewhere to hide. Most of them saw a boy standing amongst the diseased outside the palace. He wasn't infected. It made them believe he could help."

William said, "We saw that."

"You know the boy?" the hunter asked.

William shrugged. "Why are you doing this? What do you want?"

"To not die."

"Let Cyrus go and we'll move on. We don't want to stay here, and we have no desire to kill you. Just let us all go."

"How do I know I can trust you? The second I let him go, you'll kill me. I have no one left. I had one friend, and he's now dead. We got separated by the diseased. We hid in different rooms. When I got to his room, I found him in a wardrobe."

Olga looked across at William.

"That was you?" the hunter said.

William's stomach tensed. Any bargaining power had been lost in that one glance. But then he saw Max climb up onto the roof. If he could buy him time ... "Well, not exactly," William said.

"What do you mean, *not exactly?* You either did kill him or you didn't. There's no grey area."

Max drew closer to the boy, walking along the roof on his tiptoes. Thirty feet between him and the hunter with the knife. Too far away to act.

"The boy attacked me first. It was an accident. I shoved him back and he fell into the wardrobe. A peg went through the back of his head. I didn't mean for it to happen, I swear."

Tears filled the hunter's eyes and he shook his head. He trembled more than before, blood leaking from where he pressed the knife to Cyrus' throat.

Before William could say anything else, the hunter yelled and dragged the blade across Cyrus' neck. Blood sprayed away from the cut, and Cyrus went down, gasping and gargling as he fell to his knees.

"No!" Max screamed and launched his knife.

The hunter turned around in time for the tip of Max's knife to sink into his face. It turned him instantly limp and he fell to the tiles while Max screamed again, running towards Cyrus.

On his knees with Cyrus' head in his lap, Max screamed for a third time, his pain coming out of him in waves. He stroked the boy's face. But it was too late. Blood drained from Cyrus' neck and he stared up at Max through dead and glazed eyes.

CHAPTER 44

William wrapped Max in a one-armed hug, his friend's clothes sodden with sweat from where he'd dug Cyrus' grave. A few hours had passed, and all that remained of their kind friend was a small wooden cross and a mound of dirt. "Come on, mate, we need to get moving before it gets dark. It's a few days' walk to Gracie's community, and we need to find somewhere safe to spend the night that isn't here. Somewhere Matilda can rest her thigh to let it heal."

Max hadn't spoken since Cyrus had died. His voice weak, he nodded and said, "He was a good person."

"The best," William said, his throat sore with grief. A tug on Max's shoulder, he said, "Now come on." The cries of diseased in the distance, they were yet to come into view. "We need to get out of here."

William led Max away. Both of them stumbled on weak legs. Rest would do little for them now. Grief was a process. They had to keep moving. They needed to leave the palace behind them and live life one step at a time.

The sky had turned orange with the setting sun. They'd find somewhere to stay within the next few hours.

William walked beside Max.

Dianna and Hawk helped Matilda hobble along.

Olga and Artan walked side by side.

Gracie led them towards her community.

None of them spoke.

The swish of the long grass.

The caw of an occasional bird.

The tone from the palace grew distant.

Barp! ...

Barp! ...

Barp! ...

END OF BOOK SEVEN.

Thank you for reading *The Asylum: Book seven of Beyond These Walls*.

***Between Fury and Fear: Book eight of Beyond These Walls*, is available at www.michaelrobertson.co.uk**

Support The Author

Dear reader, as an independent author I don't have the resources of a huge publisher. If you like my work and would like to see more from me in the future, there are two things you can do to help: leaving a review, and a word-of-mouth referral.

Releasing a book takes many hours and hundreds of dollars. I love to write, and would love to continue to do so. All I ask is that you leave an Amazon review. It shows other readers that you've enjoyed the book and will encourage them to give it a try too. The review can be just one sentence, or as long as you like.

If you've enjoyed Beyond These Walls, you might also enjoy my other post-apocalyptic series. The Alpha Plague: Books 1-8 (The Complete Series) are available now.

The Alpha Plague - Available Now - Go to
www.michaelrobertson.co.uk

Or save money by picking up the entire series box set - Go to www.michaelrobertson.co.uk

ABOUT THE AUTHOR

Like most children born in the seventies, Michael grew up with Star Wars in his life, along with other great stories like Labyrinth, The Neverending Story, and as he grew older, the Alien franchise. An obsessive watcher of movies and consumer of stories, he found his mind wandering to stories of his own.

Those stories had to come out.

He hopes you enjoy reading his work as much as he does creating it.

Contact
www.michaelrobertson.co.uk
subscribers@michaelrobertson.co.uk

READER GROUP

Join my reader group for all my latest releases and special offers. You'll also receive these four FREE books. You can unsubscribe at any time.

Go to www.michaelrobertson.co.uk

THE ARENA
MICHAEL ROBERTSON

Michael Robertson
EDEN
A Short Story About The Zombie Apocalypse

RAT RUN
A POST-APOCALYPTIC TALE
Michael Robertson

ALSO BY MICHAEL ROBERTSON

The Shadow Order

The First Mission - Book Two of The Shadow Order

The Crimson War - Book Three of The Shadow Order

Eradication - Book Four of The Shadow Order

Fugitive - Book Five of The Shadow Order

Enigma - Book Six of The Shadow Order

Prophecy - Book Seven of The Shadow Order

The Faradis - Book Eight of The Shadow Order

The Complete Shadow Order Box Set - Books 1 - 8

∼

The Blind Spot - A Science Fiction Thriller - Neon Horizon Book One.

Prime City - A Science Fiction Thriller - Neon Horizon Book Two.

Bounty Hunter - A Science Fiction Thriller - Neon Horizon Book Three.

Neon Horizon - Books 1 - 3 Box Set - A Science Fiction Thriller.

∼

The Alpha Plague: A Post-Apocalyptic Action Thriller

The Alpha Plague 2

The Alpha Plague 3

The Alpha Plague 4

The Alpha Plague 5

The Alpha Plague 6

The Alpha Plague 7

The Alpha Plague 8

The Complete Alpha Plague Box Set - Books 1 - 8

∼

Protectors - Book one of Beyond These Walls

National Service - Book two of Beyond These Walls

Retribution - Book three of Beyond These Walls

Collapse - Book four of Beyond These Walls

After Edin - Book five of Beyond These Walls

Three Days - Book six of Beyond These Walls

The Asylum - Book seven of Beyond These Walls

Between Fury and Fear - Book Eight of Beyond These Walls

Beyond These Walls - Books 1 - 6 Box Set

∼

The Girl in the Woods - A Ghost's Story - Off-Kilter Tales Book One

Rat Run - A Post-Apocalyptic Tale - Off-Kilter Tales Book Two

∼

Masked - A Psychological Horror

∼

Crash - A Dark Post-Apocalyptic Tale

Crash II: Highrise Hell

Crash III: There's No Place Like Home

Crash IV: Run Free

Crash V: The Final Showdown

∽

New Reality: Truth

New Reality 2: Justice

New Reality 3: Fear

Printed in Great Britain
by Amazon